INTERNATIONAL RELATIONS

The Gender-Flipped Version

Parliamentary Desires Book 1

HG Jones

Parliamentary Desires has undergone a sex change! Introducing International Relations (The Gender-Flipped Version), a tale of erotic lesbianism and rampant bisexuality.

Prepare yourself to enter a world few have ever seen. A world of dark deals, Napoleonic negotiations, and salacious sex. Welcome to Parliament House.

Michelle Morgan is the number one dealmaker in the Foreign Affairs office, and her talent for securing even the hardest of agreements has not gone unnoticed. When the Minister for Foreign Affairs - Christopher Wayne - calls Michelle to his office, she knows her mission is going to take every skill she has to offer.

Does she have what it takes to save the world's largest international trade deal from falling apart? Michelle's adventure will take her from Consulate to Consulate, meeting and enticing representatives from all corners of the world. It's a task that will take her every sexual prowess, as she works her body to the bone to make sure her clients are completely satisfied.

Read the racy tale of one woman's Parliamentary Desires today.

Parliamentary Desires (The Gender-Flipped Version) is the racy, tongue-in-cheek lesbian/bisexual erotica series by HG Jones, featuring fast women, hard sex, and mind-games aplenty.

Note: All sexual acts depicted in this erotic novel occur only with consent.

Contents

CHAPTER 1 – Loose Lips and Sinking Ships

Day: Thursday
Time: 0715 hours
Location: Parliament House, Canberra

Magpies warbled in the early morning sun that shone brightly over a sleepy Canberra. The last tendrils of the overnight mist were dissipating into nothingness, revealing beads of dew, glinting like diamonds as they perched perfectly on blades of lush, green grass. There was a crispness to the air and all signs indicated there was a glorious Australian afternoon ahead.

It would have been a picturesque morning for anybody else, but there were other things on Michelle Morgan's mind. She strode in wide, confident steps across the lawn of Parliament House, not caring about the grass crushed underfoot, nor the moisture that clung to her black, pointed stilettoes. Today was not the day to concern herself with matters of that nature.

Her blonde hair – long and straight, and sensually voluminous – fluttered gently in the breeze. Her exterior, however, remained sharp and focussed. From her midnight black tight knee-length dress to her flawlessly manicured eyebrows, there was nothing to give away her emotions.

A nod was all it took for her to pass through security. It was no secret in this building who Michelle Morgan was. A woman of her nature, with her girlish charms and piercing looks was a rarity within these hallowed halls.

She knew the way to the Minister for Foreign Affairs and Trading's office like the back of her hand. There was no need for chaperones or glorified tour guides, not anymore. For several months now, she'd walked these hallways several times a week, all in the name of conducting foreign affairs on behalf of the state.

It had been years in the making, and months of work to settle the final negotiations for the ever-important Trans-Global Trade Partnership. Together, she and the Minister had met with nearly every Foreign Secretary from across the modern world, from all regions and backgrounds, all with the aim of convincing them to sign onto the final draft of the deal.

But with the negotiations closing, and the final signatures expected by Tuesday and noon, the tension had reached boiling point. While she was confident they had the numbers they required, it would only take a minor protest from a signatory to derail the entire operation. And for Michelle, she was staking her entire career on this agreement. Were she to pull it off, it would be without doubt in her mind, his greatest achievement so far in her role within the Department.

"I'm here to see the Minister," she announced loudly to the young man working on the reception desk, throwing her designer handbag at him, and strutting onward as though he didn't even exist. Michelle didn't have time for young, powerless men in business, or in pleasure. She never had, and she certainly never would.

"Ah, Michelle! You're here early," greeted Foreign Affairs Minister, Christopher Wayne.

He was a tall man, Christopher, his grey hair the only indication of his five decades on the planet. There was something steely about the Perth native, a man known for his political ruthlessness. It was his determination to succeed above all else that Michelle admired in him – they were kindred spirits in that regard.

"I'm very glad you're here Michelle," he continued, his voice low and gravelly. "I just got off the phone with the British Embassy. Those precious bastards say they need more details on the partnership before they're willing to sign off on it."

Whatever could they want now? Michelle had only spent the last week describing the deal and what the partnership would entail in great detail to the British Foreign Secretary. However, the man was an oaf at best, and it was no surprise to her that he was as clueless about the whole arrangement as he had been they day they first struck up a conversation. The memory of a goldfish, that one. Always the professional, Michelle kept a straight look on her face and her thoughts to himself.

Christopher continued on – "It seems they have a few questions regarding the size and the position that Australia would take in the partnership. All very stressful business, wouldn't you agree?"

Michelle nodded slowly. "I can see where they may have been confused. I've been negotiating with so many different people, it's hard to keep up the stamina sometimes."

"Oh, I can't imagine stamina is your issue," replied Christopher, as he slowly loosened his tie and unbuttoned his shirt. Beneath the cotton of his garment was his bare torso, covered only by a thin veil of curly hair that extended from his nipples down to his abs before disappearing below the waistband of his black pants. "In fact, I know for certain you have the best stamina of any woman I've ever employed before."

Michelle could feel her pussy moistening in her hot pink G-string as she gazed upon Christopher's perfectly chiselled body. Animalistic desire rushed through her blood. Christopher was right – there were no issues with Michelle's stamina.

She stepped confidently forward, and grabbed Christopher by the neck, passionately kissing him and reaching for his oesophagus with her tongue. Deft hands worked at Michelle's dress, unzipping it with fervour, before casting it aside in a heap on the floor. Skin to skin, they kissed passionately, tongues sliding around in one another's mouths. Michelle could feel Christopher's large hands on her body, pawing at her perfect breasts, his finger drawing concentric circles around her right nipple.

Michelle knew her thong would be soaked through with her vaginal secretions any minute now. She could feel her clitoris engorging within her sensual labial folds, begging her for liberation. With swift hands, she snapped the band of her G-string, and discarded it politely on the Foreign Minister's desk.

If there was one thing Michelle was proud of, it was her pussy. It was perfectly pink, plump and ready to take on any sized cock it encountered. But more than that, she knew how to use her impressive internal muscles and vaginal juices to leave even the most hardened of lovers moaning and gasping.

Not one to waste time, Christopher Wayne dropped his pants to reveal his cock to her. It was of average length, which she could enjoy, but thick and filled with promise of endless orgasms.

"We are definitely going to have fun today, aren't we?" murmured Michelle, as she devoured Christopher's cock, pumping slowly at it with her mouth and speeding up. There was something so sensual about having a man's manhood in her mouth, pleasuring him with all she had to offer.

It wasn't long before the sweet taste of pre-cum entered Michelle's mouth, and it only made her work harder with her tongue. She relished in the power she had over one of the most influential men in the country, possibly even the whole world. With just a flick of her lips, Michelle could have him gasping and panting for air, or bellowing with ecstasy.

Christopher let out a small groan and pulled himself back away from Michelle, before kissing her full on the mouth. She was sure to let him taste his own cock on her breath, his fluids on her tongue. There was nothing hotter in a man, in Michelle's opinion, than wanting to savour their own essence.

It energised him, and brought a new level of arousal to Christopher's body. With a firm hand, he bent Michelle over the stone coffee table in the middle of his office, and bending down, began to lick her vulva and labia. He started off slow, teasing Michelle, drawing his tongue upwards in large sweeps, before focusing in on her most erogenous clitoral zone. Thick, heavy globs of spit were smeared all over Michelle's vestibule, and trickled erotically into her vaginal canal.

He reached forward, and caressed Michelle's clitoris with his left hand, masturbating her pussy tenderly. The wedding band on his finger provided an arousing yet cooling sensation, like ice on her hot snatch.

It wasn't long before Michelle was groaning as well. "You are far too good at this for a politician," she gasped.

"The first rule of politics," Christopher replied, "is to know how to please the cunt above you." If that were true, it would explain why the Minister was such an adept politician. It was well known around the halls of Parliament House in the Press Gallery that Mr Wayne had ambitions far higher that the Foreign Affairs portfolio. There was only one way he was heading, and that was to the top.

With a thrust and a gyration of his hips, Christopher slid his cock into Michelle's willing pussy. His hand on her neck, pinning her down, the Minister thrust at her hole, plunging himself deeper and deeper into Michelle, until there was no more he could give her.

They writhed on the desk together, grunting and groaning like wild animals. She could feel Christopher's body pressed into her back, rolling his hips, sliding himself slowly in an out of her. With each thrust, Michelle could feel the tension welling within her pelvis, waiting to explode out of her. *This man is amazing,* Michelle thought to herself. *I wonder if his wife knows how lucky she is to have this?*

But Christopher clearly wasn't ready to let the encounter end. After ten minutes of thrusting and growling, he pulled his cock out, and admired the gaping mess he'd made of Michelle's pussy hole. "Get on top," he growled.

He treated her like a rag doll, and pushed Michelle out of the way, before lying flat on his back.

With a steady hand and thigh, she lifted her stilettoed foot onto the top of the desk, flashing him a glimpse of her inner vaginal folds and nooks, feeling a breeze on her trimmed landing strip from the nearby air-conditioner. She towered over him for a second, all labia and breasts, before lowering herself. With a moan, she felt Christopher's cock slide past her clitoris, and it penetrated deep into her portal once more.

It was now or never. Michelle knew this was her one opportunity to impress Christopher, and make him truly believe she had what it took to finalise the Trans-Global Trade Partnership once and for all. Then, after that was done, she'd be guaranteed a secure position within the Department of Foreign Affairs and Trading, for as long as Christopher held the portfolio.

Michelle thrust her vagina at Christopher hard and deep, feeling his pubic bone slam into her sensitive clitoris. With every ram and toss, her tits bounced on her chest, flopping about like out-of-control wind turbines. She thrust herself against him as hard as she could, faster and faster, with all the power she could muster, reaching closer and closer to blissful orgasm.

It was while Michelle was being tossed about like she was on a mechanical bull that they both climaxed simultaneously, drenching each other in the fluids of male and female ejaculation. Gasping and trying to catch their breath, they clambered off the stone desk, each of them a dishevelled wreak. Michelle's legs felt like jelly underneath her, and balanced herself for a moment while she regained her senses.

From the top drawer of his desk, Christopher pulled out an old-looking towel, and wiped himself down, before throwing it to Michelle. There were no further instructions required. Once he'd wiped every last drop of the Minister's seed from between her thighs, Christopher collected the towel and placed it back into the desk drawer.

"You'd better have a shower before you meet the British Foreign Secretary," Christopher instructed. "I'd hate for him to suspect anything was going on between us right before he signs off on the agreement". He gestured Michelle towards the door on the left wall of his office. She knew right behind it was his private bathroom, having been in there with a different staff member only days beforehand.

Michelle stepped into the shower, and let the cool water wash over her naked, exhausted body. Her moistness was finally washing away and she felt a deep sense of contentedness roll through her body. She knew Christopher was also deeply satisfied with their encounter – how could he not be? Water dripped from Michelle's slender body, ran down her perfectly tight front and dripped down from her hairless labial folds. She could feel the sweat and the raw desire being washed away, and once fully refreshed, she emerged from the shower. Taking extra care to wipe down her breasts, her thighs, and her perfectly plump pussy, she cast the white towel aside when she was done with it.

She could only hope her impending meeting with the British Foreign Secretary would be as satisfying as the one with Christopher Wayne, although she doubted anybody could match the raw physicality they'd just shared.

CHAPTER 2 - A Very British Proposal

Day: Thursday
Time: 1020 hours
Location: British Embassy, Canberra

Michelle was completely refreshed by the time she reached the Bentley parked out the front of the House, courtesy of Christopher Wayne. Her long blonde hair had dried completely and her black, skin-tight dress remained wrinkle-free. There was a nervous electricity in the air around her, as she lowered herself into the black leather upholstered seat of the car.

This would be the first time she'd met the British Foreign Secretary in person. Their previous negotiations had been via video link or phone, sometimes email, but never up close and in the flesh. She knew Leonard Thompson quite well by now, so much so, they operated on a first-name basis. From what Michelle had seen, the British Foreign Secretary was quite a handsome man, with short dark hair, delicate facial features and impeccable dress-sense. She remained, however, somewhat confused with the information Christopher Wayne had given her – Leonard still had questions regarding the size and the position of interest? *Whatever could that mean,* Michelle thought quietly to herself.

The Bentley sped furiously through the sleepy Canberra streets, zipping over roundabouts and stopping just in time for red lights. The driver was clearly taking the long route, but that worked in Michelle's favour, for she was able then to revise her notes regarding their last discussion. But the more she read, the more confused she became. The only points they'd discussed at the last meeting were in regards to transcontinental migration and joint economic goals, nothing that needed reiterating. Not really. Even an imbecile should be able to work out the legislature for themselves.

It was nearly half past ten when the car pulled up outside the British Embassy, and Michelle, who was by this point extremely unsure of the reason for this meeting, pushed open the door and leapt out. There was no point being unenthused, not when the whole deal could fall apart at any moment. She quickly gathered her handbag, and made her way across the concrete lawn and through the glass sliding doors at the entrance of the building.

"I'm here to see the Foreign Secretary. Could you direct me to his office, please?" Michelle asked the security guard at the main entrance.

He replied in a strong Scottish accent. "Take that corridor down to my left, look for the first lift on the right-hand side, and take it to level 3. That is the Foreign Secretary's private suite." Michelle thanked him politely and followed the instructions carefully. Eventually, she located the lift and stepped inside and pressed the big button next to **Level 3 –**

Foreign Secretary's Private Suite. There was an aroma of mahogany and detergent in the air, not enough to be overpowering, but enough to pique Michelle's intrigue. There was only one reason she could think of to warrant sanitising an elevator like this.

The lift swiftly raised through the building until it stopped abruptly at level thee. With a hiss, the doors opened to reveal an ornately decorated mahogany lobby. She stepped out into small reception area, where a young woman, about twenty-four years old sat patiently behind the desk.

"Hello, you must be Michelle Morgan. The Foreign Secretary is expecting you," the young receptionist said. She had an accent Michelle couldn't quite place, but it was somewhere between Irish and Cockney.

"However," she continued unperturbed, "before I can allow you in, I must perform a security check."

Oh, for fuck's sake, a security check? Michelle thought incredulously. It was as if these people existed solely to make life difficult for her in a time when she should be relaxing on a beach somewhere, knowing full-well that the deal was going to be signed, no matter what.

The young woman immediately set to her task. She took Michelle's handbag from her, and with rapid hands, began to examine her body. She squeezed Michelle's bare upper arms, fondled her breasts, and worked her hands down her front, lower and lower. When her hands reached Michelle's pubic zone, the young woman moved her hands, feeling down her back. Reaching down, she grabbed Michelle's stellar ass firmly in her hands, squeezing them once, twice, three times.

She hummed in approval. "I am going to need you to take your dress off for me please, so I may complete my security check."

Michelle obliged, knowing full well she had nothing to hide. It wasn't like she was keeping a secret explosive under there or anything. Unbuttoning the garment and dropping it to the floor, Michelle stood half-naked, wearing only a midnight black brassiere and a sapphire belly ring. The young woman once again fondled at Michelle's tits. With a cunning glint in her eye, and a smack of her lips, the receptionist gave Michelle a knowing look. "I think we have some suspicious packages here, and I will obviously need to inspect further."

Michelle could feel himself getting annoyed. If this was how the youth of today flirted, she certainly had some notes for them. Still, she took some pity of the youthful lass – it hadn't been all that long ago that she'd been just as awkward, and twice as shy with her Janes and Johns.

Without another word, the young woman had slipped Michelle's tits out of their fabric prison, and began to suckle delicately on her nipples. She could feel her pussy moistening in response, getting wetter and wetter until the young receptionist slipped a finger inside her, and massaged her clitoris with her hand.

For someone so devoid of any semblance of a personality, she was rather accomplished at using her tongue and hand to massage Michelle's tits and clit, even brushing noticeably against her G-spot deep inside her vagina.

Michelle's womanhood responded to her every manoeuvre, pulsating and quavering gently. She could feel the orgasm rising inside her like hot fire, and when she couldn't hold on any longer, she climaxed, her muscles squeezing down on the young woman's hand as she deposited her sticking saline secretions.

Pulling her fingers out, the young woman slipped them into her mouth, sucking on Michelle's womanly essences indulgently. "You can go in and see him now," the receptionist said, satisfied with her morning delivery.

Michelle immediately re-dressed herself again, for the third time that morning, and was led through the mahogany door immediately left of the reception desk. From the corner of her eye, she could see the young woman busying herself with documents and a fax machine, pretending nothing had happened.

She stepped into a large room with wood-panelled walls. Probably mahogany – everything else in this place was. In the centre of the room, facing the door was a large wooden desk, and on the far wall, either side of the escritoire were two other mahogany doors.

What a queer room, Michelle thought to herself as she gazed about. The walls and floor space were adorned with many pieces of ancient Greco-Roman art. Perched comfortably on the desk was a small stone replica of the Statue of David, which immediately caught Michelle's eye. She didn't have much time to gaze before the door on the right opened, revealing the British Foreign Secretary, Leonard Thompson. He looked younger in person than he'd appeared on the video link, perhaps in his late thirties, or early forties at the oldest. The harsh British lighting had done him no favours. It took Michelle a moment to realise he was wearing only black pants and a silken white shirt.

"Michelle Morgan, it truly is a pleasure to be in your company!" he said and a very posh, most-definitely London accent. Michelle shook his hand, and was surprised by the strength of his grip.

"It is nice to finally meet you, sir!" replied Michelle. "I am curious, however, about the need for this meeting? I was under the impression we had reached an agreement by now."

"Michelle, please. This is the first time we have ever met in person! Surely, business can wait a few minutes. Now, let us toast to this special occasion," Leonard exclaimed, snapping his fingers twice. The young woman from the reception desk entered the room with a serving trolley, covered by a silver lid. "Thank you, Maxine!" Leonard said as the young woman left the room again. Leonard lifted the lid to reveal two glasses filled with amber liquid. He handed one glass to Michelle and took the other for himself. "To a successful venture, and perhaps, the beginning of a good friendship!" he said, taking a deep swill.

Michelle sipped her drink slowly. She immediately knew from the taste and smell that this was very expensive Scotch. "Yes," she replied. "To venture and friendship."

Leonard had already finished his glass, and was busy pouring another from the crystal decanter on his shelf. "Very well, let's get to business and then we can enjoy the pleasure of one another's company, yes?" Leonard said. "I asked you here because there is something I need, and it is something I believe only you can give me."

Michelle was instantly curious.

"You see, Michelle, I come from a long line of English nobles. My family has a very rich history as you may be able to tell by the small collection of artworks I keep here in my suite. But you see, people are very envious of my family, and they have every reason to be. We are one of Britain's wealthiest, and have become wealthier and wealthier with each successive generation. Now, there have been a number of incidences – let's call them what they really are though, shall we? Robberies. My family has been robbed a number of times in the past, and thieves have made off with hundreds of thousands of pounds worth of relics and portraits. But there is one piece, one very special portrait that was stolen over one hundred years ago. It is of my sixth great grandfather, Albert Thompson, the founder of our House. It is very valuable, and carries a great deal of sentimental weight for my family. I have been very recently informed – very recently, in fact – that this particular portrait has turned up in a collection owned by the French government. Of course, they will deny this, I am certain. But, Michelle, I understand you are an excellent negotiator. I will sign our Trans-Global Trade Partnership agreement, but only if you manage to get the portrait of Albert Thompson returned to me."

Michelle was lost for words. This seemed almost an impossible task to complete. How on earth could she convince the French to return a painting stolen over a century ago? She took a deep breath in. "I'll do it," she said. "Or at least, I'll try to. I have a meeting with the French Ambassador tomorrow afternoon, so I will begin negotiations then."

"Excellent news, Michelle. I am so pleased I can entrust you with this important task," said Leonard, clapping his hands together joyously. "Now let's get down to business. I need to tell you about the British ships we'll be sending into your Australian ports."

"The ports?" asked Michelle, feeling totally confused again.

"Yes. The ports. I need to know more details. Please, take your dress off so I can demonstrate."

Slightly miffed at the number of times she'd been asked to remove her clothes for such an early hour, Michelle complied with his simple request, discarding her bra as well so that she was completely naked on the leather seat.

Leonard walked behind her and began to massage her breasts with his warm hands. He leaned in and nibbled on Michelle's ear. "I need to know that my ship can satisfy the needs of your charming port," whispered Leonard, as he moved his hands down to Michelle's stomach and began to kiss her on the neck.

"Oh!" said Michelle, realising this talk of ships and ports was all euphemism. "Well, the port is very much adequate to most desires. Would you like to see?" She stood up, and raising her leg, exposed her labial folds and vagina.

Leonard gasped. He had never seen such a perfect specimen in all of his life. "Oh my, yes!" he cried. "This will be absolutely marvellous," and immediately tore off his clothes and threw them aside, revealing his own naked body. He has a slim yet very toned figure, shortly trimmed black pubic hair and a long, uncut cock. Michelle eyed him off hungrily, feeling her insatiable appetite rising in herself yet again.

No matter what troubles befell her, no matter how awful the world around her was, Michelle Morgan knew she could always rely on her snatch to meet the challenge head-on.

She kneeled down and started to worship Leonard's cock with her mouth, doing everything she could in his power to please him. Her mouth sucked and her tongue licked every inch, revelling in the feeling of that long cock reaching the back of her throat. She could hear Leonard above her groaning with pleasure.

The British Foreign Secretary took a deep swig of his Scotch, before pouring the rest of the glass onto Michelle's head, as though baptizing her. He pushed Michelle to the floor, and pushing his cock into her mouth again, stretched himself to lick and kiss at her moist, exposed clitoris.

Michelle was shocked by the initial burn of the Scotch in Leonard's mouth against her sensitive glans, but took up the invitation to perform oral sex on Leonard anyway. The two bodies writhed on the ground together, far too caught up in the pleasure each was giving, and receiving.

There was nothing more enticing in this world than a man's tongue upon her clitoris, lapping at her trickling vaginal juices. Michelle was overcome with ecstasy, and pushed Leonard onto his back, before straddling him, penetrating her hole deeply with his penis, until it reached as far as it could go.

They groaned and grabbed at each other like two horny inmates in an all-gender prison as Michelle gyrated herself against the cock in her pussy. She made sure Leonard responded exactly as she wanted him to. With one tit in hand, she carefully stroked her clitoris with the other. Her vaginal muscles tightened around the British cock, tugging at it, pulling it until, like a geyser, they both erupted, filling her with prostatic fluids only to be flushed out by the torrent of sticky, salty vaginal ejaculate. The smell of sex and sweat hung in the air like a badge of honour, as they lay on their backs, panting as though they'd run a marathon.

"For an Australian," gasped Leonard, "you sure know how to fuck like a professional." And with that, he quickly redressed himself and left without saying another word. The moment he closed the door behind him, Michelle decided it was time she put her clothes back on as well. Once dressed, she called her driver and give him strict instructions to meet her out the front in five minutes. With a flourish of her mind, Michelle mentally rearranged her afternoon plans in her head, making plenty of time to do her research on the portrait of Albert Thompson, but also, to find out more about the mysterious French Ambassador who was in apparent possession of stolen goods.

CHAPTER 3 - The Hunt Begins

Day: Thursday
Time: 1230 hours
Location: Michelle's Apartment, Canberra

Michelle knew it would be virtually impossible to convince the French government to return the portrait of Albert Thompson. The French have always held onto anything of value, even if it was just a century old portrait of a man Michelle hadn't even heard of. She could already hear the Ambassador saying in her thick accent '*What painting? We have no interest in the desecrations of English art!*' Nonetheless, she was determined to make this agreement work, knowing she had to do whatever it took.

Back at her small Canberra apartment, Michelle decided it was time to do some real research. But first, there was more important business to take care of. As soon as she closed the front door behind him, Michelle undid the zip of her dress and slipped it off in one swift movement. She took off her black bra and tossed it aside on the sofa. She stood naked in her white wall living room, her breasts sitting pert on her chest, her nipples pink and flushed. She was sore all over from the day's rendezvous and felt absolutely spent. She was certain her G-spot would be bruised black and blue by now. Michelle was wincing in pain as she walked to the shower, but found immediate relief as the hot water washed over her body. She stood there for a good ten minutes and allowed the water to carry away all the sweat and semen from her long day of work. When the time was right, Michelle stepped out of the shower and grabbed a grey towel from a coat rack, taking care to dry each of her stunning breasts individually. Once fully clothed again, she set to work preparing for the meeting with the French Ambassador. Of course, they had met several times, but everything remained above board. She hadn't even seen the French Ambassador naked, which, as Michelle assumed, was odd for a Frenchwoman. In her experience with the French, they had always seemed open to nudity, even encouraging it. Nobody was more sex positive than the French, and even they had a habit of being too sex positive. Michelle wasn't even sure the Ambassador was a lesbian – she could have been straight, or worse, asexual! Assuming sex was off the cards, Michelle knew there was only one other way to get the painting back – blackmail. And with that, she proceeded to review the Ambassadors Wikipedia page in fine detail.

After three hours of googling and researching, Michelle still had nothing. It was as if this damned Ambassador was a saint! No scandals or incidents she could use to her advantage, not even a husband or a lover! Not even, much to Michelle's dismay, any record of the Ambassador using the services of a prostitute, male or female. The situation became all that much harder and for the first time ever, Michelle wasn't sure her ample bosom and willing vagina would be enough to get the job done. This would require careful planning and perhaps even some illegal moves. She pondered for a moment, before getting back to work. After several hours, Michelle had a breakthrough.

"Aha!" shouted Michelle to nobody in particular. "I have it!" If there was no scandal to be found, perhaps one could be created…. Michelle knew instantly how she would achieve this seemingly impossible feat – it would involve her pussy and a hidden camera. And with that, Michelle retired to the bedroom, and fell asleep within moments of her head touching the pillow.

CHAPTER 4 – French Fried

Day: Friday
Time: 0630 hours
Location: Michelle's Apartment, Canberra

Michelle rose early at 6.30am to begin her day. The meeting with the French Ambassador was not until 10am, giving her plenty of time to prepare himself for what lay ahead. It was imperative she keep up her stamina and ensure she was in top shape for the meeting, given anything could happen.

She made her way to the gym on the ground floor of her apartment building, and spent the early morning doing some core training. Michelle's body was more than just a weapon, or a commodity. It was her greatest tool, her most important method of disarming the uninitiated. In a world of hard deals and even harder sex, the composition of one's physique could make or break their ambitions before they've even begun to emerge.

There was no man or woman on earth, Michelle believed, who could resist the temptation of her rock-hard body, her vagina of steel, and her breasts that had been blessed by the gods in the highest of Heavens and the depths of Hell. To let herself go, as so many women when they reached the great age of thirty-two, was not an option for Michelle Morgan. She'd sooner lay down and die.

Beads of sweat soon collected on her bare torso and flat stomach, and pooled into her belly button. She pushed herself hard, feeling every muscle stretch and contract, so that she looked even more impressive than usual. Every part of her body was addressed, each in turn, until her muscles rippled beneath her skin.

"Looking good, hot stuff!" called a voice from behind. It was Michelle's neighbour, whom she didn't have time for and didn't even know his name. He was a short man, rapidly approaching his late forties, and judging by his physique and facial features, Michelle assumed he'd had a hard life too.

"Thank you," said Michelle, who had not forgotten her manners, before putting her jacket on again and leaving. Back in her own apartment, she had time to prepare herself for the meeting with the Ambassador. She reasoned it was all in the look, and planned her outfit down to the finest detail. First things first, the aroma of desire. Michelle sprayed herself with her favourite perfume – a mixed scent of floral bouquet and cinnamon, with a dab of honey-scented secretion from her own vagina. Irresistible. Foregoing her morning shower was a small price to pay for the feminine scent she naturally produced.

Next, the undergarments. The French were the true masters of boudoir accoutrements, and she needed to be at the top of her game if she were to seduce the Ambassador. From her top drawer, Michelle withdrew a racy red G-string that allowed every detail of her sequestered pussy to be revealed through the lacy yet durable material. It came with a matching brassiere that gave first class access to her nipples, assuming the Ambassador was a lesbian – or at the very least, a bisexual.

Over the G-string, Michelle chose to wear a black, well-fitted skirt that revealed the spectacular curvature of her ass. They say the champagne glass was modelled off Marie Antoinette's breast, and if that were true, you could model a champagne bucket off Michelle's glorious buttock.

Her shirt was white, and slightly see-through, so that her bra, breasts, and nipples could be easily seen in any light. All may be fair in love and war, but Michelle's body was the perfect weapon for both. She was unmatched, unrivalled by anybody else within her field of expertise. There was nobody in the world that could do what Michelle did, of that, she was certain.

Michelle arrived at the French Embassy at exactly 9.45am. She hadn't yet had the pleasure of visiting, and for a brief moment wasn't even sure it was the correct address – it looked like a couple of white sheds behind a security gate. "Are you sure this is it?" she asked.

"I can always tell when it's someone's first time here; they always ask the same question," the driver joked back to her. "Yes, it is the Embassy. Look, there's the flag."

True to his word, there was indeed a French flag flying above the shed at the front of the compound. It wasn't much, but Michelle had learned not to make assumptions. Sometimes sad little things could actually surprise you, and occasionally in a good way.

But there were no fancy tricks in this little compound, much to Michelle's disappointment. Not even an automatic door. Nor was there a security guard or even a doorman to operate the front door. No, it was up to Michelle herself to push open the main door with her bare hands.

"Bonjour," she greeted the bored-looking young French man at the main desk. "I'm Michelle Morgan. I have a meeting with the Ambassador."

The young man looked up, and spoke to Michelle in rapid French. "*J'ai l'air de parler anglais, putain d'idiot?*" It was obvious to Michelle that this young importee was not going to be useful in any way. He wasn't even attractive enough to consider fucking.

"Whatever, merci, jackass," sniped Michelle as she stormed away from the desk, looking for any signs that would lead her in the right direction.

Finally, she spotted a sign that read *L'Ambassadeur*, with an arrow pointing along a hallway. She looked around, expecting a security guard at least to intervene, to stop her from just walking into the Ambassador's office and making love to her until she agreed to give up the painting of Albert Thompson. But there were none to be seen. It was as if the French were poor and could not afford even the basic security required to effectively protect their assets.

She sauntered along the dimly lit hallway, reading signs on doors like *Salle à fromage* and *Objets rares*, until she came to one that read, in plain English, Ambassador. Michelle took the opportunity and knocked hard on the door – perhaps too hard, because it swung right open to reveal a bare ass thrusting away at a shocked Ambassador, who was bent over her desk.

"Go away, go away!" she cried in a very thick French accent.

Michelle tried to shield her eyes so that she didn't see any more than she needed too. "I'm sorry, I'm sorry!" she yelled into the room.

There was a scuffle of a chair on the linoleum floor, of clothes being hastily thrown back on, zips being zipped up where necessary, and heavy breathing. It would have been almost comical, except for Michelle, this meant someone else was cutting her turf. There was no way the French Ambassador would be interested in Michelle's fine qualities now, now after she'd been getting pummelled against the desk like that.

Instantly, Michelle's mind turned to suspicion. Was this a competitor, a stranger in the midst determined to snatch her victory away from her when she was so close? So close, and yet so far, it would seem.

"Ms Morgan, you're early," the Ambassador gasped in her thick accent. "Well, we may as well explain this situation and get down to business."

Michelle opened her eyes slowly, afraid of what beastly scene lay before her. The Ambassador was standing before her, with her grey print dress thankfully back on, and behind her was a gentleman fumbling around with his belt. A man Michelle immediately recognised. A man who should never have been in the French Ambassadors' office, let alone fucking her silly against her own desk.

It was in that instant, the exact moment she recognised the Ambassadors' secret lover, that she knew she had all the blackmail material required to get the painting back. This was a secret too great, too devastating for either of them to risk being leaked out to the wider world.

For the man who had been fucking the Ambassador was none other than Hans Von Fritzl, the German Chancellor.

CHAPTER 5 - Exposing Secrets

Day: Friday
Time: 1000 hours
Location: French Embassy, Canberra

Michelle was, for the first time in a long time, utterly speechless. She stood there, mouth agape, still processing the visual imagery she'd just witnessed.

"Michelle," began the French Ambassador, "we have kept this secret for a very long time, and you are the first person to expose us. Please, it is very important you understand what has been happening."

She looked panicked, and with good reason. An affair like this could spell the end of both their careers. But Michelle was a silver linings kind of gal, and she knew somewhere in this mess, was the answers to her prayers. All she needed to do now was play her cards right, and the game would fall straight into her lap, bingo.

But importantly, Michelle wasn't a stupid woman. All she needed to do was play dumb, let these two horny fools wrap themselves up in their ropes until they tripped and fell into her trap.

The Ambassador continued. "Hans and I, we have been… involved, for about ten years now. It is very secret, and nobody knows at all. It began before I was Ambassador, and before he was the Chancellor when everything was ok. But our affair endured and our deep affection for one another prevented us from ending it, even though it was the right thing to do." She paused for a moment, and looked positively crestfallen. "Yes, it has been difficult for both of us. Now that I have been posted here for the last six months things have become incredibly difficult. For both of us. But also, especially hard for Hans."

Hans wiped a small tear from his eye. "Ach, ja. Very difficult indeed, my friend. You see, it has been a long affair. And vorse, my vife, she is leaving me because I have been too busy pining for Brigitte and not fulfilling my role as a husband."

Michelle was shocked. First, at the affair, but also at how freely they were giving this information over to her. She'd had to fuck men for hours on end before, until they begged her for mercy just to get this sort of information out of them. But here they were, two fools in love, confessing everything to an Australian woman whose only crime was walking in on their lovemaking.

"Oui," said Brigitte the Ambassador. "It has been very hard. And to make matters worse, our relationship too is having problems." Brigitte had been reduced to openly sobbing. "We have spent ten years together and now we are being pulled apart. The passion is leaving our relationship. What you saw today, all this" – she widely gestured to the crumpled papers on the desk and bottle of lubricant slowly dripping water-based fluid onto the timber – "all this is my attempt to spice up the relationship."

"Ve have had our hardships, but ve are confident ve will get through this together," said the dejected German Chancellor. "For nothing is stronger than the love and deep affection between France and Deutschland."

Michelle doubted this claim, but remained silent. "Perhaps there is a way I can help," said Michelle, looking them directly in the eyes, and winking slowly. "When my friends David and Samantha had relationship troubles, they decided to have a threesome with a burlesque performer called Natalie Nips, and that really helped them out. Perhaps I could do the same for you?"

The Frenchwoman and the German looked at each other. "Vat do you think, my darling?" asked the Chancellor.

"There has always been three people in this relationship, with that blasted wife of yours hanging about. I say we do this, and we do this right now!" replied the Ambassador, hungrily eyeing off Michelle's covered breasts. Michelle was very happy to see her choice of clothing had the desired effect. The Frenchwoman stood up and walked over to Michelle, and stood behind her. She bent over and kissed her hard on the mouth, pushing the back of Michelle's head into her crotch. She was very pleased to feel the Frenchwoman's silky-smooth labia against the back of her head. Brigitte moved her hands down, and began caressing Michelle's nipples though the thin material. They responded extremely quickly, and began to harden and erect, like push-pins trying desperately to pop out of her bra and shirt. She would most certainly enjoy this.

The German, obviously feeling very aroused by this point, walked over and proceeded to undo Michelle's skirt, pulling it down completely, along with her red G-string. Michelle's pussy was revealed completely, ready for duty.

Hans set to work dutifully, caressing every inch of Michelle's labial zone with his mouth and tongue, his dark brown hair flapping limply cross her pubic region. The Frenchwoman, not wanting to miss out, unbuttoned her own dress again, and smoothly slid it off. She pulled Michelle's hands behind the chair and used a discarded brassiere to tie her wrists together. Her shirt came off, and she used the sleeves to cover Michelle's eyes, tying them into a makeshift blindfold. The red bra was removed at haste, leaving Michelle completely naked, bound and blinded.

Once she was ready, Brigitte nuzzled at Michelle's nose with her dark pubic hair, and bushed her lips with her clitoral hood. Michelle obligingly opened her mouth, and allowed all the tastes and aromas of France enter her olfactory bulb and mouth. She was salty and moist, tart but sweet as well. She expertly caressed the Frenchwoman's gash with her tongue, licking and slurping until she was certain the woman wouldn't be able to hold on much longer.

"Untie me, please," she asked. It was the German who came to her rescue, removing the blindfold and taking off the makeshift hand tie. The German man was fully naked by this point, and Michelle marvelled at his body. He was tall, taller than Michelle, with well-defined muscles and impressive abs and between his legs, a very impressive looking cock. He was cut, and long in length, at least ten inches, and appropriately thick. Hanging beneath were two impressive balls within their natural sack. Without thinking, Michelle started to lick the German's scrotum and before long, was sucking on his left testicle before proceeding to the right. Hans hummed in satisfaction, and clearly approved of Michelle's actions. Brigitte, not to be left out, stood next to Michelle and began to passionately kiss Hans deeply, reaching for his tonsils with her tongue. Michelle fondled at Brigitte's pussy, and sliding two fingers in, began to masturbate it, slowly so that she wouldn't get too excited.

It wasn't long before Michelle had Hans' cock in the back of her throat, hungrily devouring it in all its glory. Sucking on Hans' dick and playing with Brigitte's pussy at the same time was in itself extremely pleasurable for Michelle. She hadn't felt this turned on in a long time.

Hans pushed Michelle off his cock and whispered "My turn to eat you, my dear," with a devilish grin on his handsome face. Before she knew it, Michelle was laying back on the desk with her legs waving about in the air as the German devoured her cunt, licking and tonguing it until Michelle saw stars. Brigitte, not wanting to miss out, squatted over Michelle's face, and invited her to give her pussy the same treatment. There were groans of ecstasy from both Michelle and Brigitte, signalling to Hans that it was time to change tactic. He stood up, bent over Michelle and kissed her on the mouth, pushing his tongue deeper until it reached places his cock had been only minutes beforehand. He pressed firmly on Michelle's vaginal lips, and pushed one finger inside her. Feeling along the edges, he quickly located Michelle's prominent G-spot, and began to expertly massage it with one finger, before adding a second finger and a third into the situation. Michelle felt the tension in her pelvis, but didn't allow herself to climax. Not yet, anyway. Suddenly, Hans slipped his large penis into Michelle's accommodating vagina, and thrust deeply once, twice, three times… Brigitte got on top of the desk and straddled Michelle's pubic zone, scissoring their clitorises against one another. Three bodies thrust and writhed together for several minutes, as they all moaned and groaned. Michelle could feel an enormous orgasm rising deep in her pelvis, stimulated by both Hans' cock in her pussy and Brigitte's clit on her own …. Groaning loudly, Michelle shuddered as her orgasm flushed through her body, pushing the two others to orgasm as well. The room was filled with animalistic noises and the sound of three sweating bodies pounding each other vigorously. Panting, they lay there briefly before untangling themselves and getting themselves back together again.

"I think," gasped Michelle, still panting hard, "I think that was the best sex I've ever had in my life!"

The other two agreed. Indeed, for all three, the sex was the best they'd ever had.

Once fully dressed, the trio sat down for their scheduled business meeting. Brigitte began. "Michelle," she said, "I understand you have gotten me here to finalise the agreement you are hoping to make with me on our respective nation's behalf. And of course, after than performance, I am very willing to agree to it. In fact, there's not a lot a won't agree to after that." She quickly scrawled her signature on a stack of forms and handed them to Michelle.

Michelle knew she had to take her chance now. "Thank you, Brigitte, that is very helpful of you. Now, I must ask for one more thing. I met with Leonard Thompson yesterday – the British Foreign Secretary. Now, he is also on board with this deal, but he will not sign until the French government return a portrait of his ancestor, Albert Thompson to his possession."

Anger flushed across Brigitte's face. "Of course, he thinks that French art belongs to him! Of course, that British worm accuses us of theft, without acknowledging the thefts by his own blasted nation!" She continued to rage in rapid French for several minutes before Hans was able to calm her down.

Michelle decided to take a gamble. Afterall, the agreement had been signed and there wasn't much to lose. "I respect that Brigitte, really. But I too have a secret I have kept from you. I brought with me a recording camera, and have streamed our lovemaking to a secret hard drive. Now, that painting is all it will take for that footage to remain on that hard drive. But if I don't get that painting by tomorrow evening, unfortunately that video may be leaked to every news organisation in the western world." Michelle was deadly serious, and the two diplomats sitting before her could tell. They could barely hide the look of fear that spread across their faces.

"You have a deal, Australian," said the Chancellor slowly. "You know this video could destroy not only my career, but my entire country too. I cannot have that. Germany has always been united and I cannot risk destroying that now! You will have your painting; I will courier my copy of the Trans-Global Trade Partnership agreement to your office. And then I hope we never see you again!"

Michelle was satisfied with the outcome. Both France and Germany were on board, and by Tuesday evening, she could count on the British to have signed onto the agreement too. That meant there were only six more people needing to sign up and she would have orchestrated the biggest international agreement of the modern times.

Once fully clothed, she left the Embassy with an air of satisfaction. It was a shame that her afternoon of incredible sex ended on a sour note, but Michelle wasn't bothered much. She had always hated the French, and the Germans weren't much better in her book.

CHAPTER 6 – The Fat Man

Day: Friday
Time: 1230 hours
Location: Parliament House, Canberra

Michelle strolled back into Parliament House and immediately proceeded to walk to the office of the Foreign Ministry. But before she reached the elevator, a voice called out after her. "Michelle! Michelle! Oh Michelle, the Minister for Agriculture needs to see you regarding section 18C of the trade agreement immediately!" Michelle was surprised, as she had never even met the Minister for Agriculture before. If anything, it was directly between Minister Wayne and the Minister for Agriculture to work out their own arrangements with this deal. Doing as she was told, however, Michelle immediately steered herself in the direction of the Minister's office.

After several minutes of walking, Michelle knocked on the enormous mahogany door, and awaited a reply. The door opened, to reveal a tiny, older woman. *This must be his secretary*, thought Michelle.

"Who are you?" she demanded in a very thick Australian accent, or rather, as Michelle identified correctly, a very North Queensland accent.

"I am Michelle Morgan, and I have been asked to see the Minister!" she replied, firmly but politely, much like her own pussy.

"Indeed, you are," she replied. "I'll take you through to his office." And with that, Michelle followed her into the Minister's office. She was immediately surprised by the bareness of the room. It was unlike any other office she'd seen in all of Parliament House. There were no book cases, only a small desk with very plain chairs either side and a hideous photo, at least six-foot-tall, plastered on the wall behind the desk. The photo featured a man, a very fat man, draped in an Australian flag, with a rusty chain hanging limply over his shoulder. The photo was taken from the side to enhance the projection of his enormous gut, and it was very clear that he was both naked underneath the flag, and that he also appeared rather aroused, given his erection protruding from his groin. His piggy eyes squinted out from under a layer of blubber, as if to say 'I love my country more than you could imagine'.

Michelle was immediately repulsed, and fought the urge to vomit. But there wasn't time for further gazing, as suddenly the Minister had appeared. He looked exactly like he did in the enormous photo, but instead was wearing an Australian flag tank top and a pair of very tight, white shorts. Michelle could tell he wasn't wearing underwear.

"You must be Michelle," said the Minister, in the same North Queensland accent as his secretary. "My name is Doug Perry. Well, Michelle, we do need to have a chat about the Trans-Global Trade Partnership agreement. Now, on review, I have noticed that one of the sections discusses beef trade with the Americans; 18C, I believe. Do you really think we are going to allow the Americans to sell beef to us here without any import fees? No! We have our own bloody farmers here struggling to rub two one hundred dollar notes together while those fucking Americans are rolling in riches!" The minister was very angry, and his enormous stomach was wobbling with rage. "Explain that to me!" Doug demanded.

Michelle wasn't sure if Doug Perry was being belligerent, or was simply stupid. It wouldn't have surprised her. There was only one way the most stupid Members of Parliament fell, and that was upwards.

"Well sir," started Michelle, "I did not formulate that part of the agreement…" She continued on, before Doug rudely interrupted.

"I want it removed!" he bellowed. Michelle knew this would take some very delicate negotiating and she knew just the way to do it.

"I'm very distracted by that wonderful photo on the wall" she said. "It's exquisitely stunning."

"Thank you!" said the Minister. "Yes, that was one of my proudest moments. That photo was taken right after I managed to catch and kill a wild boar with that very chain. I am so proud of this country."

"You certainly seem very proud," said Michelle. "I am thinking of getting a Southern Cross tattoo myself actually," she said, to the Minister's apparent delight. "I'm thinking of getting it right here," she continued while taking off her shirt and pointing to her right shoulder blade.

"That is a good spot, but mine is better," replied the Minister haughtily, taking off his shorts and exposing his bare ass. On the left buttock and extending up to his gelatinous love handles, was his very own Southern Cross tattoo. Turning around, Michelle also saw an Australian flag in the shape of a love heart tattooed on his very inner hip, just next to his dark and curly pubic hair. His penis was beginning to harden. It wasn't very big in length, but it was certainly very thick, just like the Minister himself. "That feels much better," Doug exclaimed, breathing a sigh of relief, and placing his hands proudly on his hips. "I'm a nudist myself, Michelle. All good Queensland men are nudists."

Michelle shuddered. The way the grotesque man kept eyeing her up and down, as if she was to become his next kill, just like the boar. Surely not. Surely, Michelle would not be able to fuck this man, no matter how hard she fantasized about someone, or even something else.

"You look like you'd enjoy a bit of nudity too, eh?" Doug continued, his enormous backside wobbling like underset jelly. He gave Michelle a wink that sent tidal waves of revulsion through her body.

Even for a professional, Michelle was caught off guard. She didn't expect this meeting to go this way. She knew it was going to be hard to maintain her professionalism in this situation. After considering all the options, Michelle realised she had only one choice – she had to fuck Doug Perry, and fuck him good enough to make sure him change his mind about section 18C of the trade agreement. Breathing deeply, Michelle readied herself for what could potentially be the worst shag of her life, even worse than that time she had to screw the Leader of the Opposition while his wife watched on.

"Yes," said Michelle calmly. "I do enjoy some nudity." She was secretly hoping this would be the end of the conversation.

"I knew it!" exclaimed Doug, eyeing her off again. "Allow me to assist you," and began to undo her bra. Michelle stood still, allowing Mr Perry to enjoy his moment. Before long, Michelle's shirt and bra were on the floor, and the Minister began to lick and grope her glorious breasts and nipples. Michelle was not feeling aroused just yet, but desperately hoped her vagina would get in the mood soon. The entire trade deal could depend on her sexual performance right there in the Minister for Agriculture's office.

Glancing around the office, Michelle happened to spot a photo of another nude male on the shelf next to the Minister's desk. She was keen to get a closer look, hoping it would provide some visual inspiration for her clamped vaginal lips. Fortunately, she didn't have to wait long. Doug seemed satisfied with Michelle's chest, and proceeded to work his way around, groping, grabbing, touching her back and her shoulders, seemingly finding the best place to grip her. In these movements, Michelle was able to lean over the desk and get a closer look at the photo. The man in the photo was quite handsome, and very slim, not muscled, but proportionate. He looked to be in his mid-twenties, perhaps twenty-five, twenty-six at most. Michelle felt the blood rush to her clit, and knew, no matter what happened here, she had to think of that photo at every moment.

Before too long, Doug set to work on Michelle's trousers, unbuckling and tugging at the belt buckle, and impatiently pulling down the zipper at the front, exposing her groin. Doug stood up, and took a step back to marvel at his work, and after a brief moment, Michelle's black trousers fell down, leaving her fully exposed again. The Minister smiled gleefully to himself, beaming like the Manchester Cat, which for copyright purposes is nothing like the Cheshire Cat. Doug eyed Michelle's naked body up and down, and appeared satisfied with what he saw. Michelle distracted herself by thinking back to the photo, although she didn't want to look at it, lest the Minister see it was not him that Michelle's body was performing for.

"Yes!" cried the Minister. "I can see you really are a nudist! That body is stunning, absolutely magnificent! Much like myself when I was younger," he cried, gesturing towards the photo on the shelf. Michelle was shocked, although refused to let it show. The man in the photo, was that really Doug Perry? Surely not! Although… the eyes were the same, and, as she looked closer, she noticed that they had the same cock! She had an excellent eye for the male genitals, and never forgot a penis. Much like a jeweller checking over a diamond, Michelle was certain the two penises were the same. Yes, that was Mr Perry in the photo! But how did he get like this? So fat? It didn't matter. Michelle knew that one, the fat man before her looked like the man in the photo, and two, that was enough to get the oestrogen flooding into her loins.

Doug sensed Michelle's arousal, and lunged at her. He kissed and playfully bit her neck and ear while slowly but deliberately stroking and fingering her clit. *He has very soft hands*, thought Michelle, and allowed herself to give in to the experience. She could feel Doug's own cock thrusting into her thigh, and knew it was time he started to get to work. She looked Doug square in the eye, and began the jerk his member off. "You had better be prepared for an experience with me," Michelle whispered in his ear. The Minister seemed to be pleased with this, and immediately shuddered and climaxed on Michelle's thigh.

Doug groaned loudly, and collapsed to the floor. *Wow,* thought Michelle, *I must be better than I thought!* Doug continued to groan and gasp on the floor, and was grabbing at his chest. But, as Michelle quickly realised, the man on the floor was having a heart attack! She has quite literally given the Minister for Agriculture the orgasm that killed him! Immediately, Michelle set about performing CPR on the fat man, hoping he would survive. Afterall, the trade deal could sink if the Minister was dead. After beating at the man's chest for several minutes, there was a shudder, a shake, and suddenly Doug let out a cough. He was alive!

"You saved my life, Michelle!" he said. "How could I ever repay you?"

"Well, you could start by leaving section 18C of the trade agreement alone".

"What?" asked Doug. "What 18C? What agreement?"

"You know, the one you requested I come to your office for."

"I don't remember any agreement, or why I asked you to come to my office."

Michelle pondered for a moment. Yes, Doug had been unconscious for several minutes. It was certainly possible he was suffering from memory issues now. Perhaps, just maybe, possibly, he had no recollection whatsoever, and this could be Michelle's saving grace. "Minister," she began, "before the ambulance gets here, I just need you to sign off on one document for me please, it won't take long. It is just in regards to the sale of some livestock to the United States." She held her breath, hoping she hadn't helped jog Doug's memory.

"Of course!" said Doug. "Anything for you!"

Michelle reached into her designer handbag and found the contracts. While Doug was busying himself signing several pages, Michelle composed herself, got dressed, and called security to alert them to the health scare. Before long, the ambulance had arrived to take the Minister to the hospital.

"Michelle," whispered Doug, as he was being loaded onto the gurney. "Michelle, I want to give you one last gift. The photo above my desk. The one of the naked man. Please, take it. Let it inspire the nudist in you to be free."

For the first time that day, Michelle was truly touched, and this time, it wasn't in the pussy. She walked of the office feeling very satisfied, despite not having orgasmed and still feeling sexually aroused. There would be time to take care of that later that day. For now, though, Michelle knew the trade deal was within her grip, and knew within days it would be signed, and she would be paid a handsome sum for her efforts.

CHAPTER 7 – America's Finest?

Day: Friday
Time: 1347 hours
Location: Michelle's Apartment, Canberra

Michelle made it home in the early hours of the afternoon, at exactly 1.47pm. By now, she had a serious case of blue flaps, and was in desperate need of an orgasm, or maybe three. As soon as the door slammed behind her, she tore off her shirt, ripping the buttons from their attachment points. The trousers received the same treatment. Dressing fashionably yet professionally had its drawbacks, and she made a mental note to stick to wearing short dresses where she could gain easy access to her pussy in times of desperate need. Michelle stood alone in her living room, fully naked, with her semi-aroused nipples hardening in a dignified way. Thinking back to her interaction with Brigitte and Hans, her cunt became flushed and roused. Michelle begun to toy with her clitoris while standing in her living room, tensing and relaxing her vagina rhythmically.

Feeling more and more turned on, her hands became more and more adventurous, roaming across her labia and finding their way to her pulsating hole. She began to walk, still rubbing her moistening clit, towards her bedroom. In the top drawer she found her favourite vibrator, pink and smooth. After a few moments of fiddling, Michelle was hunched over on her bed, ass up in the air, with the buzzing device lodged firmly in her vagina. She massaged and stroked her clit again, slowly, and taking good care to get her fingers all the way down along her labial folds. The pulsations in her pussy threatened to push her over the edge, but Michelle held on, knowing it would be worth it. She continued to rub her clitoris, speeding up and slowing down, getting ready for the explosive orgasm welling up inside of her. She reached around with her left hand, and began thrusting at herself with her vibrator, while furiously beating at her clit with her right hand. The orgasm was bubbling inside, and Michelle rolled over, legs spread in the air. She couldn't hear the sound of the buzzing coming from her pussy over the noise of her heavy breathing. She was thinking back, a long time before, to another man, one she had loved and who had loved her in return, although no more. She thought of the way she used to lick this man's body from head to toe, and began to lick her own lips, not sure where fantasy ended and reality began. She was close now, and her strokes became more powerful, forcing the orgasm within to erupt from the surface. With a deep groan and an arching of her back, Michelle let the orgasm come forth, squirting a small amount of acrid vaginal juice from her snatch. Gasping, she removed the still buzzing toy from her pussy, and rolled over once again, so that she was lying on her stomach. Nearby, she heard her phone buzz and ding, alerting her to an email she had just received. The email read:

Attention staffers,

There will be a meeting at 6pm today at Government House as a measure of goodwill for our esteemed foreign guests. This meeting is compulsory for all staffers working on the current trade deal.

6pm. That would give Michelle enough time to shower and recuperate, and hopefully give her vagina a chance for a rest, if this were to be the kind of meeting that required her sexual skills to negotiate.

The drive to Government House took twenty-three minutes, and Michelle spent this time wondering what the meeting could be about. She concluded it was a congratulations on having all the small details sorted out, and to celebrate the signing of the document by all the official members of the trade agreement. She felt content that she, and her irresistible pussy, had managed to bring the deal together. Before long, the car had pulled up outside Government House and Michelle was ushered inside. The foyer was filled with dignitaries of all nationalities, many of whom Michelle had engaged with in various ways during the negotiation process.

"Michelle, dear girl!" a voice called out. It belonged to Leonard Thompson. "Michelle," he said, siding up beside her. "Michelle, I don't know how you did it, but I just received word from London that the painting is being delivered as we speak!"

"I don't know what I did, but I know who I did," said Michelle, winking with her right eye.

Leonard replied "Oh, the Frenchwoman and her German lover? Yes, yes, we all know about their affair. I suspect they are the only ones who aren't aware we all know! Even the German's wife knows about it all. Now, let's talk business. I am satisfied with all of the arrangements thus far, and I have decided, with the backing of my government, of course, that I will sign your trade deal."

Michelle was very pleased, and smiled to herself. "Well, I don't have the contracts with me at the moment, but I will arrange to have them couriered over to your office, first thing in the morning, if that suits you?"

Before Leonard could reply, a noise rang out from the main entrance. It sounded like someone choking on a pretzel, or perhaps a piece of German bratwurst. "Ach! Michelle Morgan!" It was the German Chancellor, Hans Von Fritzl. "Michelle," he said, quieter this time, as he was now standing next to her. "Vat did you do this morning? Brigitte has left me! I vill not be signing your devil documents until you convince her to come back to my embrace!" And with that, Hans stormed off, leaving Michelle speechless yet again.

"Looks like you've got more work, or should I say, more men to do!" said Leonard, with a chuckle.

But that was the end of the conversation, because a bell rang out, indicating hors d'oeuvres and beverages were to be served in the main dining hall. By this point, Michelle was desperate for something stronger than a cup of tea. She followed the crowd into the main dining hall, where topless waiters, wearing only bathing attire by a popular brand were serving canapes of all sorts. Michelle immediately walked towards the bar area, and ordered a champagne, and "a glass of something stronger too, if you have it". She was served her champagne, and a glass of dark whiskey over a few ice cubes. She downed the whiskey in one go, and started to sip on the champagne slowly. *What should I do now?* Her deal was falling apart right at the moment she thought it had all come together. All the training she'd put herself through, the countless hours of learning the art of negotiation, the extraordinary number of sessions she'd spent in the gym – none of that had prepared her for this moment. She gazed out into the room, eying off the dignitaries and staffers who were present. Craning her neck, she searched desperately through the crowd for Brigitte. That was, as far as Michelle could tell, the only way to get this deal back on the cards. She kept scanning the heads and faces of the guests until, there, in the back corner, was Brigitte. She was in deep conversation with a woman with very short hair and a tight red dress, who had her back turned to Michelle, although judging by the structure of her ass, was about the same age as her. *This is it*, thought Michelle. *This is my moment again.* She walked over casually, coughed a little, and said "Excuse me, may I have a word?"

The mysterious woman turned around, and for a moment, Michelle was shocked, although she did her best to hide it. The woman talking to Brigitte was none other than Charlotte Adams, the American Diplomat's chief of staff. Michelle had a lot of dealings with this woman, who had pulled the American's out of the trade deal in the early stages of setting it up. This lady, and the people she represented, had caused Michelle a great deal of grief only a few months prior, when the trade deal had to be rebuilt from the ground up. This, however, was the first time seeing her in person and not over video link.

"Michelle Morgan," Charlotte said, in her southern American drawl. "I see you've been busy with my new friend here!" She was quite good looking, with defined facial features, deep brown eyes, and light brown hair, with a touch of ginger running through. She was also quite tall, standing about six inches or so taller than Michelle.

Michelle started to panic. She knew what was happening. Charlotte, like most Americans, was intent on destroying good deals for the rest of the world for her own amusement. *I have to do something!* Michelle thought. "Yes, I've been very busy satisfying the needs of everybody in this room. Now it's time for Ms Ambassador here to satisfy my needs."

Charlotte's face flushed with rage, and the Ambassadress looked around for an immediate escape. Michelle was beginning to suspect she hadn't anticipated being the pawn in the game between two arch rivals.

"We are talking here, Michelle," Charlotte started. "Fuck off and stop being so rude." The Ambassador nodded with agreement. This wasn't going so well for Michelle.

She knew this wouldn't work out for her, and decided it was time to try a different approach. "My apologies, I'll be off and I might catch you during the evening." She turned, and walked back to the bar, knowing full well that the American was trying to bring the deal apart. It was time to reassess the situation, and devise a new plan. When she reached the bar, Michelle asked for another whiskey. This time she sipped it slowly, savouring it, and appreciating the flavours. It was smoky, a bit spicy, with a hint or vanilla and caramel. Michelle had an appreciation for whiskey, and immediately recognised this was a southern American-style. It was in this moment that Michelle knew how to get to the French Ambassador. But before she could, Christopher Wayne, the Foreign Minister, took to the stage.

"Good evening, ladies and gentlemen!" he started. "Good evening and welcome! For several months now, all of us here in this room have been hard at work putting together a trade deal that will benefit all of our nations. And I am pleased to say we are in the final stages of drafting the deal, with only a few nations left to sign on. So, I propose a toast, to all of you, who have made this vision a reality!"

Michelle noticed Charlotte scowling in the corner as everybody else in the room raised their glasses and murmured their approval.

Christopher continued: "This evening is an opportunity for you all to enjoy yourselves! There will be no further business." And with that he stepped off the stage to rapturous applause.

Peering through the crowd again, Michelle noticed Charlotte was alone once again. She understood that the only way to get to the French Ambassador again would be through her. Michelle went back to the bar, and this time requested two whiskeys. She carried the glasses through the crowd, making her way to Charlotte.

"Hey Charlotte," Michelle started, "I think we got off on the wrong foot a few months ago. I hope we can work past that now and come to a better understanding." She offered one glass of whiskey to Charlotte.

"Well, I don't usually drink on the job, but I could make an exception for you, Michelle." Charlotte took a sip of the amber liquid, and gasped. "Oh, my Lord, this is exactly the same whiskey Ma fed us when we were kids!" She gulped the last of the glass down in one swift movement.

"How about I get you another?" Michelle asked, and made her way back to the bar without waiting for a response. Her plan seemed to be working after all. She returned with two more glasses, and before long, Michelle and Charlotte were roaring with laughter like old friends. They made their way through several glasses of whiskey in only two short hours.

By now, Charlotte was visibly inebriated, and she turned to Michelle and said, "If you like whiskey, there's a great selection at the hotel I'm staying at. That's if you're up for a real introduction to Southern culture."

Michelle hadn't prepared for this possibility. But she knew she had to do whatever it took to get to Brigitte, and if that involved spending part of the evening with Charlotte, then so be it. "I would love that," said Michelle, trying not to let the numerous whiskeys cloud her judgement.

Before long, the two of them were in a taxi making their way to Charlotte's hotel.

CHAPTER 8 – Charlotte's Web

Day: Friday
Time: 2130 hours
Location: The Mad Monk Motel, Canberra

When they finally arrived at the hotel, Michelle had decided she would have sex with Charlotte, if it came down to that. After all, Michelle was insatiable, and her clit and tits knew all the right things to say. Charlotte led the way to the hotel bar, which was an ornate room, with a wooden saloon-style counter in the centre of the room. Several brass chandeliers lit up the space, providing excellent mood lighting.

"I think it's my turn to get a drink, don't you?" asked Charlotte, her Southern accent becoming strange and distorted with her drunkenness. She ordered for them, and two glasses of deep brown whiskey were served over ice cubes. Michelle took a sip, and was surprised by the burn.

"Wow, that is strong!" she said, gasping slightly.

"It tastes much better this way," replied Charlotte, and she leaned in and kissed her hard on the mouth. Michelle could taste the whiskey on her tongue, and had to agree, that it did taste better this way. Charlotte was an excellent kisser, and knew exactly how to get Michelle turned on. Both of their pussies were moistening in their respective G-strings. Michelle was surprised at how aroused she was, especially given the history between the two. *Or perhaps*, she thought cheekily, *that is exactly why I'm so wet right now.*

Charlotte had moved from kissing Michelle on the mouth, and was making rings with her tongue on Michelle's neck. She could barely keep her aroused breasts in her dress. Before long, her heaving chest ripped through the fabric, exposing her tits and nipples to the whole bar. Charlotte didn't seem to mind though. She took another sip of whiskey, and began to lick at her nipples, when she snaked her hand up Michelle's dress, and pulled her thong aside to finger the moistness of her womanhood. Another sip of whiskey later, and Charlotte's head disappeared into Michelle's dress too, licking and suckling on her aroused clitoris. The burning sensation of the whiskey was matched with a cooling feeling – Michelle realised Charlotte had an ice cube in her mouth as well. Michelle found herself tangled in the intoxicating web of ecstasy, and had to push Charlotte away lest she came too quickly.

"You taste goooood," Charlotte said, in a seductive manner with her Southern accent. With a swift movement, she pulled her dress halfway down her body, exposing her bare torso and breasts to everyone in the establishment. Michelle was, to say the least, impressed with her physique. It was clear to her that Charlotte knew her way around a gym as well as she knew her way around Michelle's own body.

Michelle began to lick and play with Charlotte's nipples, much to the American's delight. With the first shudder of her chest as she began to groan, Michelle quickly tugged the rest of her dress down, revealing her seductive clitoris nestled within a triangular thatch of trimmed pubic hair.

She was so hungry for her, more than she could have realised. Perhaps more than she should have been. It was a dangerous game to fraternise with the enemy, and Michelle Morgan had a death wish.

She began to stroke Charlotte's vulva with her hand, slipping a finger inside and masturbating her gently yet firmly, using a bit of saliva as lubricant. There had never been a more perfect twat at her hand – except for her own, of course. What a shame it was, what sweet sorrow that Charlotte was, and would always be his nemesis.

Charlotte tugged at Michelle's dress, forcefully undoing the zip, and pulling it down her body, completely overcome with unquenchable desire. She was a beast if ever there was one, a woman who promised to fuck the living daylights out of Michelle, two, maybe three times over. With deft hands and swift movements, Charlotte ripped Michelle's dress straight off her body, leaving it in tatters on the floor behind her.

"I don't come to Australia often enough," said Charlotte. "And I've never heard of you coming to the States".

"I haven't needed to go to the States in years," replied Michelle seductively. She purred like a lioness, luring her prey to herself, ready to pounce and strike.

"Play your cards right, and you might just get an invite."

Michelle knew her plan was working. The thing she'd learned about women, especially alphas like Charlotte, was they all wanted to be tamed. Sometimes that meant tying them up and spanking them, and other times it meant seducing them with all the charm and sexuality she kept in her body.

Charlotte was clearly no longer thinking about the trade deal, or Brigitte either for that matter. Her eyes were fixed firmly on Michelle's physique and her ladyhood. This pleased Michelle a lot, and the mere thought of it made her vagina release a couple of lubricating droplets into the edges of her lower lips. Sometimes she even surprised herself with how well she could negotiate deals using her sexual prowess.

Before long, Michelle had Charlotte's clit in her mouth, and was sucking and slurping at it, lapping up every droplet of sensual womanly moisture from it. She was aromatic, like a desert in the spring, and her cunt juices tasted of rainwater after a heat spell.

Michelle was ravenous, and Charlotte was proving herself to be quite the buffet. With every movement, Michelle felt herself getting more and more aroused. This may be the most wet she'd ever been in her life! Unable to take any more, Michelle released Charlotte's engorged clit from her tender lips.

She searched through her bag quickly, and pulled out a long, purple silicone dildo. "Fuck me with this," she moaned seductively into Charlotte's ear, before laying back on the bar counter, and spreading her legs wide so that the American had a perfect view of everything she had to offer.

With a brute thrust, her gash gave way to a feeling of absolute ecstasy, as Charlotte pumped at her pussy with the sex toy. She moaned and groaned, louder and louder, and the only way to shut her up was for Charlotte to straddle her face, filling her mouth with her muff. Every guest in the bar was watching them, but Michelle didn't care. The crisp sounds of her tongue lashing at Charlotte's clitoris echoed loudly through the venue to the horror and delight of onlookers, depending upon their persuasions.

Both women were dripping with sweat and other moistures, and the aromas of sexual pleasure filled the air. It felt like they were no longer in a bar, but somewhere else, somewhere were only the two of them existed. Michelle could feel Charlotte's pussy pulsating in her mouth, and knew she was about to climax. Without saying a word, she guided Charlotte's hand to her own throbbing clit. With a few rubs of her firm fingers, Michelle shuddered and orgasmed, squirting her climactic essence all over the counter top. Charlotte followed soon behind, cumming right into Michelle's mouth. For a few brief moments, both women existed only in their respective orgasms, before coming back to reality and realising they had just fucked each other in a well-lit, public venue.

"We'd better go back to my room, before they call security," Charlotte whispered into Michelle's ear. They gathered their clothing, and made their way to the elevator. "Well, Michelle," she said once they were safely in elevator and away from prying eyes, "I can see why you are the best negotiator around. As for my earlier offer, you are more than welcome to come and visit the United States whenever you like – I'll even show you around!"

Michelle smiled. "I think I'll have to take you up on that offer."

The elevator reached Charlotte's floor, and the two of the stepped out into the hallway, and proceeded to make their way to the room. Once inside, Michelle dared to take her chance. "So, what were you are the French Ambassadress talking about?" she asked.

"Oh, that? She was telling me that Mrs Von Fritzl, the Chancellors' wife, told her to stay away from her husband. She was feeling upset and didn't know what to do."

Ah, thought Michelle. *I got it wrong… And then I must have had sex with Charlotte for no reason!* But she wasn't upset. Sometimes good sex happens for no reason at all.

Seemingly overcome by whiskey and exhaustion, Charlotte collapsed on her bed, face down, still fully naked and began to snore peacefully. Her bare ass was facing towards Michelle.

"Now there's an ass I won't forget," whispered Michelle to herself. But now it was time to get back to the plan. Realising her own dress was destroyed beyond repair, Michelle took Charlotte's discarded red number, surprised to find it was a perfect fit! She admired herself in the mirror for a moment, relishing in the way her tits and ass looked in the dress, before making her way back to the hotel lobby. *There might still be time to have a word to the French Ambassador,* Michelle thought to herself.

CHAPTER 9 – Die Scheidung

Day: Friday
Time: 2323 hours
Location: Government House, Canberra

Late in the evening, a taxi rolled quietly to a stop outside Government House. Though bruised black and blue, Michelle had recovered from her bar-side romp with Charlotte. The drive over had even given her time to sober up, even if only a little bit. She knew from experience – and common knowledge – that these political parties often continued into the early hours of the morning. And lo, she could see through the window that the lights were still on. There were even party guests dancing in the foyer to the sounds of an elderly British crooner and former sex icon. Michelle walked, staggering slightly, up the driveway towards the main entrance.

It was immediately apparent to her upon entering the House that about half of the guests had already left. Those who remained were in for the long haul. Sprawled about the main lounge, draped over various chairs or on the floor, were half-a-dozen exhausted patrons, none of whom Michelle recognised. They must either be staffers, or low-ranking officials. Someone had spilled an entire glass of red wine on the curtains, leaving a burgundy trail running down the sun yellow fabric. On the staircase, midway up to the next level, a youngish man and an anonymous woman fucked noisily, each of them emitting loud groans with every thrust. But she wasn't there to pay attention to the venturesome couple. No, Michelle was here for one person, and one person only – the French Ambassador.

The dining hall felt like the appropriate place to start searching for Brigitte. Afterall, they'd already spent a large portion of the evening within those four walls, and there wasn't very far she could travel. A topless waiter, with slightly tattered swimming garments, was holding onto a silver serving platter, offering guests one last glass of champaign, with all the dignity she could muster. Michelle graciously accepted a glass from the young woman. She'd managed to get an American to fuck her with only a few whiskeys, imagine what she could get a Frenchwoman to do with a few champagnes? And so, she began to hunt for the French Ambassador in Government House.

There was only one partygoer in the dining hall that Michelle even recognised. Hiding unsuccessfully behind a marble statue of Captain James Cook, the Foreign Minister of New Zealand and another topless waiter – bottomless too, by the looks of things – were kissing passionately. Michelle suspected this may be how the other waiter's bathers had been torn and tattered. In the far corner of the room, kneeled a woman in a black dress, who's head had disappeared up the dress of another woman. But still, the Ambassadress was nowhere to be seen.

"Excuse me," Michelle asked one of the waiters. "Have you seen the French Ambassador anywhere?"

"You mean Brigitte?" replied the waiter in what sounded like a Brazilian, or Portuguese accent. "She went up the stairs with a woman."

A woman, thought Michelle. *I wonder who that could have been.*

Michelle went back to the main foyer and began to ascend the stairs, stepping over the young couple, who were still fucking vigorously.

Once on the landing, she thought she heard the sound of a woman sobbing. Michelle paused for a moment, and used her excellent ears to detect from whence the sound was coming. Craning her neck left and right, she followed the sound down the hallway, listening in through every door she passed. Finally, she found the room the sounds of sadness were coming from. Pressing her ear to the door, Michelle made sure to listen in carefully to the private conversation taking place inside.

"He is my husband!" wailed a voice from inside. It was laden with a thick German accent, and Michelle knew instinctively it belonged to Mrs Von Fritzl, the German Chancellor's wife.

"We are in love, and we want to get married," came another. This time, the voice was that of the French Ambassador, Brigitte. She was pleading with her, begging for something, but for what, Michelle did not know.

Another pitiful wail erupted through the door, and Michelle decided then and there that this was as good a time as any to open the door, and interrupt whatever conversation was going on inside.

Mrs Von Fritzl was sitting on a desk wearing a very small, and very tight, bright blue dress. She looked like one of those women Michelle has seen in the Amsterdam shop windows in the red-light district, but was, in her opinion, far less sensuous. Brigitte was still wearing her yellow gown, though had lost the red belt from around the waist region. In the corner, barely even visible, Hans Von Fritzl was half sitting, half slouching on a chair, clearly unconscious. Both the Chancellor's wife and Brigitte turned to look at Mike.

"Who is this!?" cried Mrs Von Fritzl. "Another one of your fuck friends? I bet she's married too!"

Michelle could see the Ambassador stuttering to get her words out, and felt it was time to step in. "Not at all, Mrs Von Fritzl. I'm a negotiator for the trade deal. But I do know Brigitte and your husband too. And I can say, that yes, they are very much in love."

Mrs Von Fritzl started to wail even louder, and the Chancellor stirred in his slumber. "I thought it was over!" she cried, her words barely understandable through her accent. "I thought this was all done after the last time! I can't do this anymore, I'm leaving!" And with that, Mrs Von Fritzl stormed out of the room and down the stairs, her wails growing more and more faint like a banshee disappearing into the night.

"What have I missed out on?" asked Michelle with a wide grin.

"Well," began Brigitte, "I came up here with Hans to talk about his wife, and the next thing I know, she's up here too, screaming and acting like a *femme aliénée*! She found out about us tonight, and demanded I stop seeing Hans. I tried to end it with him, but I couldn't…. And now, I think she is the one who has ended things."

Michelle was still confused by the situation. "So, you and Hans are back together?"

"Now that, I do not know yet. He had too much to drink and has, how you say, *évanoui*… passed out. Thankfully, I think he missed all that commotion with the *démentiel* wife."

"What has he told you about his wife?" asked Michelle earnestly.

"Not very much," replied Brigitte. "All I know is that she is a harlot and a, how you say, *gold-digging whore*. She wasn't even supposed to be here. But of course, the meddling wench flew here, first-class no less, to shame her husband like this. She will do anything to keep him in her talons."

Michelle struggled to take it all in. "What do you think she will do now?"

Brigitte fought for words for a moment, then replied, "I hope she will get on the first plane back to Allemagne. But I know that is unlikely. She will do her best to create trouble for us, no doubt. She is a vile witch of a woman."

The German Chancellor stirred in his sleep, murmuring something incomprehensible, or something in German. Michelle sympathised for him – life can be difficult when you leave your wife for another woman, not least of all the French Ambassador to Australia.

"Well, I'm sure he could do with a good night of rest, and perhaps a decent breakfast in the morning," said Michelle.

"Oui, yes. He can stay at my residence with me and we will sort this mess out together. Thank you, Michelle, for your hard work for the both of us."

By the time Michelle left the party, she was absolutely exhausted, physically, mentally, and most importantly, sexually. She was going to return back home for a good night of rest and relaxation. Tomorrow was Saturday, and there was nothing left for her to do on the trade deal as far as she could tell.

CHAPTER 10 – Breaking Boundaries

Day: Saturday
Time: 0800 hours
Location: Michelle's Apartment, Canberra

Michelle awoke at 8am – later than usual, but understandable given her adventures the previous night. Stirring in her inertia, aches and pains flared anew across body where she'd been penetrated numerous times over the previous days. She was a glutton for punishment, Michelle was, and despite the castigation that had been inflicted upon her, she was always up for more.

But she was not a young woman anymore, and not even Michelle was immune to the delayed retributions that came with a night of indulgence in whiskey and maniacal sex. The hangover was unpleasant, but not completely unexpected.

She hauled himself out of bed and with shuffled steps, manoeuvred herself to the shower. The warm water did no favours for her abused tits and clit, nor her pounding headache. Perhaps it was time to give her body a rest, at least for a day.

The bitter smell of hot coffee soon filled her humble home, and she sat outside on the balcony, watching the silver gulls flying in circles over Lake Burley Griffin while she sipped on her morning beverage. If there was a better place in the world to live than Canberra, she hadn't yet found it. There was a peacefulness that came with the breeze that rustled through the eucalyptus leaves, and the fragrant aroma the tea trees released on warm summer nights.

It was the moment she finished his coffee that her phone begun to vibrate noisily on the wooden table. It was an unknown number, but Michelle answered anyway. In her industry, anyone and everyone had access to burner phones to use as needed. It was imperative that she answered all calls as politely and as professionally as possible.

"Hello, Michelle Morgan," she answered.

"Michelle, it's Charlotte. I didn't notice you leave last night. I had to call the office to get your number."

"Oh, yes, well I didn't want to intrude, so I went home."

"Well Michelle, I had a great time with you last night, and a had a great fuck. Matter of fact, it was the best darn fuck I've had in a long time. Hey, I was thinkin', maybe we could have a look over that trade deal once more. I reckon I could get the President on board with a few tweaks here and there. Whaddya say?"

Michelle was shocked. The US withdrawal had made things very difficult for her over the past few months, but this was her opportunity to show the Government, and the world, what she and her pussy were capable of. "I think I could set aside some time to negotiate," she replied coolly.

"Hey, awesome girl, what about we grab a drink later on and chat about it some more. And besides – I didn't get to finish tasting all of you last night."

The phone hung up. Michelle hadn't expected this at all. Perhaps instead of going to the gym, she should prepare some arrangements for any possible US trade deal. She sat down at her computer, and after closing several internet windows, started to review the US trade arrangement that had been drawn up months ago. But reading though the pages and pages of details, all she could think about was getting fucked hard by Charlotte the night before, and cumming harder than she ever had in her life. She smiled to himself, and her snatch gave a weak flex in her shorts. "Not yet, girl," she said. "We'll fuck her again later, and this time, even harder."

After several hours of work, Michelle believed she had the trade arrangement finalised. She just needed to clear it with Christopher Wayne, and then she could be on her way. She spent several minutes writing her email to the Foreign Minister, and as soon as she hit 'send', started to fantasise about the fantastic sex she and Charlotte would have this afternoon. Not only what would happen, but *where*. If Michelle has learned one thing from the previous night's fuck fest, it was that Charlotte was more adventurous than any of the numerous lovers she'd been with before. Sex with Charlotte could be the most exciting thing Michelle had ever done. She was hooked on the thought. Her cunt grew moist in her shorts again, and she was desperate to finger herself until she came. "Not yet," she said to herself. She wanted to show Charlotte everything he had to offer her, and then some.

After what seemed like an eternity, the Foreign Minister replied:

'Nice work, Michelle. Yes, I agree with that offer, I think it is very appropriate and hopefully enough to get the Americans on board again. But watch out for Charlotte Adams — I've heard she knows how to negotiate a

hard deal, just like you. Stick to your guns and don't offer more than we can afford. I'm counting on you here. Do <u>whatever it takes</u> to get the deal nailed."

Things were looking up for Michelle. The promise of a 'job well done' hung brightly in the air around her. But there were only days left until the Trans-Global Trade Partnership was due to be signed, and time was fast running out. She would need to get Charlotte and her bosses to approve any changes very quickly if there was any hope of getting them across the line in time.

With the flourish of fingers across a phone screen, Michelle tapped out her message to Charlotte. *Meet me at Kimono's Bar at 1300 hours.* Every part of her plan needed to be delicately balanced against the infinite possibilities. There was — as there always is in business — the chance everything could fall apart right at the last second. It was up to Michelle to ensure she was able to recognise every threat that came her way, and knew precisely how to neutralise them.

When the time came, she left her apartment wearing a tight white dress that showed off every part of her anatomy, from her tits to her ass. Her underwear was black and double-thick, protecting all her womanly virtues against erotic mishaps. Though she and Charlotte had only had one meeting together so far, she knew she'd need all the support in her undergarments that she could manage.

Kimonos was one of the finest bars in Canberra. It was a treat for visiting dignitaries from all over the world to sit between the delicate paper lanterns and artificial cherry blossoms while sipping on lychee martinis and imported beers. Mr Kimono himself, one of Michelle's many former lovers, had hand-built the venue from the ground up, and it now sat proudly on the hill overlooking Commonwealth Avenue, directly to Parliament House in the distance.

In her usual style, Michelle arrived at exactly 1pm. "I'll call you when I'm ready – this could take a while," she said coolly to her official driver, before closing the door behind her and walking over the stepping stones of grey amongst the sea of black pebbles, her glittering silver stilettoes clacking with each step.

Charlotte Adams was already at the bar when Michelle arrived. This told her two things. The first was that unlike most Americans Michelle had encountered, Charlotte was capable of being on time to a meeting. But the second inference she gleaned from her premature arrival was that Charlotte was keen and willing to do anything to get into Michelle's underpants once again.

"Charlotte, thanks for meeting me here," Michelle greeted, extending her hand professionally to her American counterpart.

She looked refreshed, her entire appearance defying the fact she'd been blind drunk and passed out only the night before.

Charlotte didn't respond verbally, but instead kissed Michelle deeply. Her vagina gave another involuntary twitch in her black panties. At this rate, she would struggle to maintain her composure long enough to nut out all the amendments that the Americans required. But now was not this time to let her sexual appetite get in the way of what could be the most crucial negotiation she'd partaken in over the last six months.

"How about we get to this trade deal first, then play later," Michelle suggested, maintaining her composure.

"Playing hard-to-get, are we?" asked Charlotte playfully. "You've already got me wet."

Michelle glanced down and sure enough, there was smell of vaginal arousal coming from her nether regions. A rush of unspeakable acts she wanted to perform on her ran through her head. How was she going to survive this meeting without ripping her dress off and going to town on the American's body?

"Best we get this out of the way quickly, then."

They set about discussing and signing off on billions of dollars' worth of trade, in between negotiations of sexual play.

"I'll sign off on amendment 2b," started Charlotte, "if you let me lick your tits until you scream".

"And I'll agree to 4h if you finger my pussy while sucking my clit," Michelle replied.

"7d is a big one," winked Charlotte. "You're going to have to make it worth my while if you want me to sign off on that."

It was by far the hottest negotiation Michelle had ever undertaken. The erotic anticipation built up in her body with every new promise they made, every stroke of the pen across the page, and every devilish counteroffer. Blood pumped through her veins, carrying with it all the hormones of desire and raw sexuality. A tricked of sweat rolled down her forehead to her brow. It was taking every ounce of Michelle's self-control to keep herself from giving into temptation, especially while their respective vaginas were both so wet in their loins. She just wanted to touch it, to stroke it and rub it, to lick it with her tongue and bathe in her moistness.

They worked themselves up, gasping on each other's tantric breaths, pushing faster and faster through their transactions. But finally, just as Michelle wasn't sure how much longer she'd be able to hold on, they reached the final page.

"Just sign it," moaned Charlotte, the impatience in her voice emanating throughout the empty bar.

"No," replied Michelle with a smirk. She'd been brought up with the belief that if there was a job worth doing, it was worth doing properly. She glanced down the page at some of the amendments the Americans had put forward. Cuts to tariffs, removals of certain export taxes, and a clause to do with intellectual property. "The Minister won't agree to any of these."

"Who cares? He's not going to notice any of them anyway; he'll be too busy congratulating you on getting the job done and the deal signed."

Michelle paused for a moment. She was torn between pleasing her boss, and pleasuring Charlotte Adams. With a pen, she crossed out four of the amendments, leaving three on the page. "Agree to this, and I'll fuck you on the Prime Minister's desk. That's my final offer."

She could see the look of concern on Charlotte's face as she read through the cancelled amendments. With a raised eyebrow here, a frown there, but forever a swamp in her panties, she contemplated the offer on the table before her. For two agonising minutes, she tapped her pen to the page, as though almost about to sign, then pulling herself back from the brink.

"Pleasure doing business", said Charlotte wryly, scrawling her long signature across the page.

"The pleasure is just about to get started," Michelle replied, with a wink.

This time, Michelle grabbed Charlotte, and kissed her hard on the lips. For all the build-up, she needed to ensure the payoff was worth it. She reached for the depths of her oral cavity with her tongue, and with every moment, became more and more aroused.

There was something about Charlotte that turned Michelle on in ways she hadn't experienced before. *Maybe it's because this is so forbidden, or maybe it's the chase*, Michelle thought.

"We should get out of here," Charlotte whispered, sending tingles along Michelle's spine. "You're going to take me to the Prime Minister's office."

There was a car, big and black, already waiting for them outside Kimono's. It took only a moment for Michelle to realise Charlotte had notified someone at the Embassy to collect her. Before the car had even started to drive, Charlotte was busy kissing Michelle on the neck and stroking her pussy through the fabric of her black undergarments.

"What, is this a Southern tradition or something?" asked Michelle seductively.

"Where I'm from, being gay is frowned upon, so we need to find places to have sex without being caught."

"So, you are gay," mused Michelle. She could tell by Charlotte's short haircut and masculine features that she was far from heterosexual.

Charlotte responded by unzipping Michelle's dress. "I'll fuck a man for business," she replied coyly. "But when it comes to matters of pleasure, it's strictly clitly for me." With expert hands, she pulled Michelle's breasts from the confines of her bra, and sucked sensuously on her nipples.

Michelle concurred. Although she was bisexual herself, there was something intoxicatingly erotic about women. Men were useful for a fuck, to feel a cock between her thighs and to pound her slender body until she climaxed, but women…. Women knew how to truly love her, to touch her innermost parts and awaken her entire body to the power of the female orgasm.

She gasped at the pleasure of Charlotte's tongue on her breast. With every flick of her tongue, Michelle felt her labia getting more and more aroused. If she kept going, they would find themselves in unstoppable territory.

Michelle pushed Charlotte's head from her breast, and slipped them back into her bra, before kissing her on the mouth again. She could have taken her right there and then, in the back of the SUV, but no, she had a promise to fulfil.

By the time her dress was done up again, the car pulled up to a stop outside the famed white colonnades of Parliament House. It was a Saturday after all, and during the non-sitting week of Parliament, so the Prime Minister and his team of staffers would no doubt be out and about somewhere in suburban Australia, chugging back beers and promising the world to any idiot that didn't have to good sense to walk on past.

"I suppose you'd like the grand tour," she asked, as they were flagged through security without any further questions.

"As long as I get to tour your body a bit more…" replied Charlotte, biting Michelle's earlobe for good measure.

"Well, come with me," Michelle purred in response, leading her through the hallways and corridors of the famed building, until they reach the sign.

OFFICE OF THE PRIME MINISTER OF AUSTRALIA

It was of no surprise to Michelle that the door was unlocked. Despite all his big talking about national security, the Prime Minister had very little regard for the security of his office. Any foreign agent could walk right in there and go through any sensitive documents they wanted. But she didn't care so much about that. No, she was now on a mission to get Charlotte Adams out of her clothes and her ass in the air.

The room was cluttered with cabinets and documents. In the middle was a large desk, and above that, a photo of the Prime Minister with the Governor General, on the day of his swearing into office. The Prime Minister was a mean old man, with a demonstrated history of homophobia and generalised hatred of anybody who wasn't a cis-gendered, heterosexual white male, preferably of British descent. In Michelle's opinion, this was the perfect place in all of Parliament House for two women to fuck each other unashamedly until their bodies were spent.

As soon as Michelle had locked the door behind them, they started right back where they had left off, tearing at each other's clothing. It was a race to get one another naked in the shortest amount of time possible. With competitive flurry, they stripped each other down to the bareness of their skin.

Not wasting another moment, Charlotte pushed Michelle back onto the Prime Minister's desk, and her head between her thighs, performed cunnilingus with exhilaration and passion. Keeping her waiting for this long was well worth it. Michelle writhed with the pleasures of Charlotte's mouth.

She was half-terrified they would be discovered, and half-excited at the same prospect. She'd be out of a job for sure if they were caught, but that was nothing compared to the need she felt for Charlotte's body pressing against her own, skin to skin, sweating as they grinded and grunted against one another.

The lashings of Charlotte's tongue on her nerve endings sent her into wild overdrive. She had fantasised about this all morning, and was not disappointed in the slightest.

"You do taste good," murmured Charlotte.

Michelle could swear there was static electricity zapping her along her exposed skin. A more perfect lover, she hadn't found in her entire adult life.

"Let's cross off some of those agreements we made this morning," Charlotte whispered, spanking her playfully on the ass cheek. With deft hands, she slipped a finger inside, and began to stoke Michelle's G-spot, massaging her exposed clitoris with the other.

It only took her moments until she had Michelle gasping for air and silently begging for mercy. One wrong move, and Michelle's pussy would explode violently, cumming all over the Prime Minister's desk with her feminine fluids.

It was Michelle's turn to work over Charlotte. She started by licking and biting at her wide, dark nipples, and masturbating her pussy with her hand. Just like a magnet, she found her head move continually southwards, until she was licking at Charlotte's moist snatch once again. She was an addict, and American pussy was her vice. Charlotte bellowed out a moan of pleasure.

"Hey, you'll have to keep it down, or we'll be caught," reminded Michelle with a laugh.

After several minutes of oral play, Michelle reached into her handbag, and pulled out a sizeable strap on dildo. Hoisting it to her hips, and noisily buckling the leather straps, she smirked to herself. "This won't hurt a bit," she cooed, before thrusting at Charlotte's vaginal opening.

"Oh god!" Charlotte groaned.

Michelle revelled in the feeling of her hips thrusting at Charlotte's, her silicone phallus sliding through her accommodating cunt, burrowing deeper and deeper into her body. She fucked her slowly, pressing herself into her vagina, past before withdrawing again. With hard, heavy thrusts, Michelle slapped her pelvis into Charlotte's buttocks, and felt her whole body jerk forward, only to be met with a groan every time. She loved teasing her, promising to pound her with the full ferocity of her body, but always holding back, even just a little. Keeping her on the edge, keeping the anticipation building.

But the thing with anticipation is it becomes harder and harder to resist, and before long, Michelle was fucking her at full velocity, pounding her cunt so quickly and so hard that Charlotte was gasping and writhing on the desk as though she were possessed. *Possessed by my prick*, thought Michelle to herself.

Reaching down, she slipped her fingers beneath the leather straps, and masturbated her clitoris furiously, and in time with her thrusts into Charlotte's body. Before long, she could feel herself ready to come. The desk was slick with sweat, and several documents were sopping wet and torn the shreds by the friction.

But still, Michelle refused to stop. Not yet. Not until she'd gotten what she wanted out this. They were frenzied, both of them, grabbing and clawing at each other, driven onward only by their desires and unquenchable lust.

Michelle pulled back, and without another word, undid the clasp and let the dido, glistening with Charlotte's wetness, drop to the floor with a thud. She climbed atop the desk straddling Charlotte, and with delicate fingers, caressed her vagina and masturbated her, groping at her breast with the other hand.

Not missing a beat, Charlotte mimicked her, sliding several fingers into her accommodating snatch, stroking her G-spot and clit with tantalising accuracy.

She groaned quietly, existing only in that moment, enjoying every microsecond, before prodding at her, faster and faster. She leaned forward, over Charlotte, looking her straight in the eyes, and could feel her matching her movement, so they were fucking each other in perfect unison, right there on the Prime Minister's desk. Michelle didn't need drugs to feel as high as she did right then.

With gasps and groans, they climaxed together, their vaginas dribbling their ejaculate onto each other's fingers, filling the air with the scent of lesbian lovemaking.

The women lay gasping in the pool of sweat they had created, delirious from their second fantastic fuck. It was rare in the negotiations business to have one great fuck, let alone two!

Exhausted, they lay there together for what seemed like hours, blissful in their orgasmic haze. Outside the office, the sky was beginning to turn a bright pink, indicating that the sun was setting.

"I think it's time we get heading off," whispered Michelle, almost afraid to break the spell they seemed to be under. Charlotte agreed, and they made their way back to the main entrance of the building.

Michelle felt elated. Even if she never saw Charlotte again, she was glad to have had the opportunity to have a filthy, ungodly orgasm right on the Prime Minister's desk.

CHAPTER 11 – Drama Down Under

Day: Sunday
Time: 0745 hours
Location: Michelle's Apartment, Canberra

Michelle woke up with morning sun streaming in through her bedroom window, catching her in the eye. Beside her, lay a peacefully sleeping Charlotte Adams. She blinked her eyes several times as she tried to piece together the events of the previous afternoon.

After fucking in the Prime Minister's office, they'd gone out to another bar, where they managed to have a few too many drinks together. *Drinking two nights in a row? That's not like me,* thought Michelle. Stretching her mind further, she recalled them going back to her apartment together, but couldn't remember anything else. Still, she wasn't going to complain. There was something pleasant and refreshing about having Charlotte around. For the first time in a long time, Michelle thought she might have found someone worth more than a root and boot.

The mood was quickly shattered by the sound of Michelle's phone ringing on her bedside table. It was

Christopher Wayne. *What the fuck does he want on a Sunday?* Michelle thought angrily. She answered anyway.

"Hello?" she croaked.

"Michelle, it's Christopher here. I'm at the House right now. There's… There's been an incident." He suddenly hushed his voice low, as though someone were listening in on his conversation. "Somebody has broken into the Prime Minister's office and fucked on his desk. Do you know anything about that?"

Michelle hesitated for a moment, in half panic, and half cool calculation. She could be honest and own up, but that would mean losing her job, and meaning Charlotte would be deported back to the US. Or, she could pretend not to know anything at all about the alleged incident.

"I only ask, Michelle, because you signed in at 1553 hours, and there's no record of you signing out."

Lie. "Well, yes, Minister, I did sign in there yesterday. I was with Charlotte Adams. We had finished with those contracts and I wanted to store them in your office before we went out together for a few drinks. You understand it's important to keep highly important documents like those protected at all costs, not like the last time when someone sold a briefcase full of them to the media." Michelle was trying not to give away her game. In all her years on the job, with all her education and training, she knew how to remain calm under pressure. She controlled her breathing, and made sure she didn't speak any faster than she normally did. That would give away her panic, as would speaking at a higher pitch. *Control your breathing, control your voice.*

"We left only a few minutes later, and were waived through by security. I presumed they'd recorded us leaving, but I suppose not."

"Ok Michelle, I knew you weren't involved. Whoever was, though, will be caught. There's a forensic team here now, taking DNA samples from the desk and the office. The PM is furious, and let me tell you now, heads will roll when he finds who was behind this!"

The phone cut out, leaving Michelle with another hangover, and a reeling head. She thought she was about to vomit. No, she really was about to vomit! She leapt out of bed and made it to the bathroom just in time. The sound of her heaving must have woken Charlotte, because the next thing Michelle knew, she was standing behind her, holding her hair back as she chundered into the porcelain bowl.

"C'mon now, I know I'm not a looker first thing in the morning, but I'm not that ugly!" she said with a laugh.

"No," said Michelle. "It's not that…" She informed her of the situation.

Charlotte stood with her arms crossed, leaning against the sink basin for a few moments. "Well," she said, slowly, making her Southern drawl even more pronounced. "Well, it seems to me we have a situation on our hands. Now, both of us are good at two things – negotiating and fucking. Maybe we could team up and use one of both of those skills to get us out of this mess?"

Michelle pondered for a few moments, mulling it over. Could they pull it off? They would have to find the investigator, and somehow use them to drop the enquiry, or even implicate someone else… She started to form a plan in her head. Yes, it would take all of her skills, and Charlotte's too, to pull this off.

"One more thing," started Michelle, "last night –"

"We didn't have sex, if that's what you're asking," replied Charlotte quickly. "You wanted to, but you were too drunk to consent."

Michelle's heart gave a little flutter. It was so rare in this world, almost unexpected, to find someone who cared about boundaries and acted appropriately when faced with a situation of uncertainly, especially when it came to the nature of sexual intercourse. The world could so with more Charlotte Adams, she thought to herself.

Together, they finalised their plan in the back of the taxi as it trundled through the suburban streets. Once completely satisfied they knew what they were doing, they instructed the driver to pull up at the service entrance of Parliament House.

With Michelle's instructions in her mind and a set of keys in her hand, Charlotte exited the vehicle, and made her way through the camouflaged doorway. There wouldn't be any security at the service entrance on a regular day, but especially not on a Sunday. And even on the off-chance there had been someone stationed there, they'd have been the first to be called from their post to assist with whatever investigation was currently taking place in the Prime Minister's office.

As for herself, Michelle followed standard protocol and entered from the front, flashing her ID as she went in. She needed to find out who was the chief investigator in the case, and made an immediate bee-line towards the destination. They say criminals always return to the scene of the crime, but this time, Michelle had a reason to be there.

As she got closer to the office, there was an increasing hive of activity in the hallways. Security guards were busy giving statements to investigators, as staffers shared their disbelief with one another. Would they suspect her, the always-loyal Michelle Morgan?

Standing directly outside the open door was a woman, young, and with red hair tied up in a bun, wearing the grey FORENSICS uniform. She could sense the golden opportunity, but for one significant stumbling block – the woman in question had long fingernails. It was the first indication that the red-haired woman was not a lesbian. The second, a Crucifix she wore around her neck. It was clear the forensics woman was in a league with the Prime Minister. Michelle would have to use her mind instead of her pussy on this particular problem.

"Hello," she said, approaching the woman. "I'm Michelle Morgan. I was in the building yesterday and wanted to see if you needed information from me."

"Well, Michelle," she replied efficiently. "It looks like two people have had a sexual rendezvous here in this office. I've taken some samples and they're off to the lab now for assessment. I still have a few hours here to clean this mess up and investigate further. I hope we find who desecrated this sacred space with their unholy activities!"

Michelle pretended to look shocked. "When did this happen?"

The woman quickly scribbled some notes down on the clipboard. "It's not an exact science," she explained, "but the heat signatures on the desk, in particular from a significant butt print, my estimate is it occurred at around 1900 hours last night."

"That's after I left," replied Michelle quickly. "I went to a bar, and here, look, I even have the time I picked up the tab," she urged showing her the transaction statement on her phone.

"Hmmm, a $340 tab at seven-thirty. You must have been at that bar for hours," she gasped.

"Yes," replied Michelle, wondering how she'd spent so much money on booze without even realising it.

But the young woman only scribbled a few more notes on her paperwork, before immediately stepping back into the office to take another look around. "That's all I needed, Ms Morgan," she said. "I'll be in touch if I need anything else."

She walked back through the corridors, avoiding the regions that security tended to focus on, sneaking through the secret passageways until she was back in the main entrance of the building. Without warning, her phone started to vibrate in her pocket. "Charlotte, what do you have for me?" she answered.

"There was a forensics car parked in the loading bay out the back. Nobody was watching it, so I had a look around and found some samples inside. I took them, Michelle.… They don't have the samples anymore."

She breathed a sigh of relief, only if for a moment. She was off the hook now, and the only evidence of her supposed crime had been erased. But then she realised they'd need replacement samples to avoid another investigation, one that would definitely land her in hot water. But her mind was already ticking through all the options. A sperm sample was needed to truly exonerate them, and she knew just where to get one.

"Charlotte, wait there for me. I'll be there to see you in a few minutes. And grab a few more specimen jars. We have some old friends to visit."

CHAPTER 12 – The Fucked and the Furious

Day: Sunday
Time: 1220 hours
Location: French Embassy, Canberra

The drive to the French Embassy only took a few minutes, but it felt like a lifetime to Michelle. This was her last chance, her last opportunity to clear her good name by framing someone else for her crimes. It was of no surprise to her that the Embassy was again completely undefended by security guards, and the two of them were able to walk right in.

"This way," whispered Michelle, pointing down the hallway where she'd walked only a few days before. Together, they tiptoed their way along, careful not to make a noise. Everything they were up to relied on the element of surprise.

Two voices echoed from the Ambassador's office, and Michelle instinctively knew they belonged to Brigitte and her lover, German Chancellor Hans Von Fritzl.

Michelle hesitated before opening the door. Her last meeting with these two hadn't gone so well, and they probably wouldn't take so kindly to her bursting in on them now.

"You do it," she whispered to Charlotte, stepping aside from the doorway. "The Frenchie seemed to like you more at the party. Maybe you can work your charm and get her to, um, help is out with a sample..."

Charlotte considered it for a moment. "No, we both go in. This is our mess, and we need to clean it up together. Besides, how could they say no to the two of us?"

She did have a point, Michelle realised. She raised her hand and rapped her knuckles on the wood three times, being sure to remain as polite as possible. The voices inside immediately stopped muttering, and a chair scraped across the ground.

It was Hans who answered the door.

"Oh, I vos not expecting to see you two today," he said with a smile. "Please, please come in!"

Michelle and Charlotte exchanged nervous glances before following the German's request. If they only knew what they were about to attempt, the European duo would have them thrown out on their asses once more, barred forever from stepping foot on their holy soil.

"Oui, Michelle and Charlotte! What a pleasure it is to see the two of you again," Brigitte beamed from behind her desk.

"A pleasure indeed," replied Michelle, recalling their incredible threesome just days before. She prayed silently to nobody that they wouldn't ask about the specimen jars that were obviously stuffed in the pockets of their jackets.

"Ve vere just, ah, talking about you, Ms Morgan," said the German, with a cheeky grin. "Our *geschlechtsverkehr*, if you will."

"I hope I left you with a good impression", said Michelle seductively. "And by the way, I find Germans are the most attractive of all people on Earth," she whispered directly into Hans Von Fritzl's ear, so that only he could hear it. This clearly had the desired effect, as Michelle noticed the Chancellor's cock give a small twitch in his pants.

"And you," said Brigitte to Charlotte. "You, I have been thinking about a lot now..."

Michelle was amazed at how well their plan was coming together. They needn't have been stressed or worried at all. If anything, the opposite. There was no way they couldn't pull it off now. Not with their combined skill and determination. Together, anything was possible for Michelle Morgan and Charlotte Adams.

Without saying a word, Charlotte undid the buttons of her black blouse, opening the front to expose her stomach, cleavage, and plump breasts.

"*C'est magnifique!*" gasped Brigitte.

That was all it took. Within the blink of an eyes, all four of them were completely naked, pussies moist and cock erect, ready for all the action they could handle. Michelle let her instincts take over. An encounter like this required all the intuition she could muster up, and she gave herself over to the spirit of sexuality the resided within her womanly frame.

She dropped to her knees, licking up the slit of Brigitte's French vol-au-vent, while Charlotte toyed with her gash from behind. Not one to miss out on the moment, Hans occupied himself by copying Michelle, and licking at Charlotte's pussy while playing with his own cock. In between moments of pleasure, Michelle looked at Charlotte, and gave her a wink. Their plan was working out well, so far.

Before she knew it, Michelle's fingers were knuckle-deep into the Frenchwoman's delicious snatch. No doubt, it had been quite a while since she'd had such dextrous and feminine digits inside her, given the state of the German's manhood.

Charlotte repositioned herself, kissing Hans on the mouth, tasting her own juices on his lips.

He should count himself lucky to have someone of Charlotte's calibre put her tongue down his throat, Michelle thought jealously. It was clear to her that Hans enjoyed the pleasures of Charlotte's kisses, given the way he was slowly stroking himself.

But how could Michelle resist Charlotte's clitoris, when it was exposed and waiting for her to give it the treatment she so deserved? While she fingered Brigitte, Michelle wrapped her lips around the Charlotte's clitoral hood, suckling her as if to say *'you're mine, don't forget it.'*

On they fucked, four of them twisting in the new positions, new combinations. Hans' face in Charlotte's pussy, Charlotte's tongue in Brigitte's mouth, Michelle's fingers plunging deep into Hans' anus. They thrashed and struggled against one another's bodies, fingers and tongues in all orifices and more.

Moans grew into groans, and groans grew into grunts, and grunts grew into screams of ecstasy and pleasure. Charlotte was busy straddled over Hans, slamming his cock and balls to her dainty hole, face red with sweat and breasts slapping against her chest, while Michelle finger fucked Brigitte in her chair, masturbating French clit with her hand. Their eyes caught, and Michelle and Charlotte gave each other a knowing look – go time.

Careful not to draw attention to herself, Michelle pulled out the specimen jar, and after carefully unscrewing the yellow lid, prepared herself for the final act. She looked at Charlotte. Charlotte looked back at her. Wordlessly, they began to fuck their respective sex dolls as fast and as hard as they could manage, determined to bring them to orgasm. With a shudder and an utterance of something in French, Brigitte's vagina clamped down on Michelle's finger, and they climaxed simultaneously. It took all of her strength and will, but as Michelle's vagina squirted a torrent of female ejaculate, she made sure to catch some of the Frenchwoman's own vaginal fluid in the specimen jar as well.

"Well," gasped Michelle, wiping her mouth, and pulling her fingers out of Brigitte's now gaping cunt. "I think we had best be off."

"I don't think they heard you," said Charlotte, tapping a slumped over Hans' on the shoulder. "Out cold."

Michelle was astonished. She knew how to give a woman a powerful orgasm, sure, but to completely knock someone out like that? This was a new skill she never heard of before, but one that would be sure to come in handy again one day.

"We should get out of here, before they wake up," Michelle whispered, as she gathered her clothes again, and dressed herself.

Michelle sighed with relief at the sight of the forensics van still parked in the loading bay. No wonder investigations in Parliament House never turned up any conclusions, not when they were always so careless with evidence. Anybody could have swiped those samples from the van, and the forensics team would have nobody to blame for themselves for their sheer carelessness.

"I'll check that the coast is clear," said Charlotte quietly, before disappearing into the darkness of the dimly lit undercover parking area. Not even a footstep was heard from her, as she traversed the perimeter, carefully watching from each angle with military precision. It was clear to Michelle that there was far more to Charlotte than met the eye.

Moments later, she returned breathing ever so gently that Michelle saw her emerge under the palest of light before she heard her.

"We're good to go," she mouthed into Michelle's ear, sending tingles down her spine and making her clit twitch in her G-string.

Now it was Charlotte's turn to plant the new samples in the spot she had stolen them from. She carefully put on woollen gloves, and checked the doors of the van. "No good," she mouthed to Michelle. "It's locked!"

Fuck, thought Michelle to himself. Their plan was to be ruined because these forensic investigators remembered to lock their van. She instantly took back every negative thing she'd thought about their team. Perhaps they weren't quite as unprofessional as she'd accused them of being only minutes ago.

"Not to worry," Charlotte reassured her. "First thing they teach you at American summer camp – always carry a multi-function knife." From her pocket, she pulled out what looked like a wooden waiter's friend. With a flick and a twist, a flathead screw part emerged, as deadly as a knife, but as subtle as a paperclip. "This should do the trick," she whispered, before darting back to the van. Through the shadows, Michelle could see her twisting at the door with the tool, and surely as day follows night, the door slid open noisily.

Heart pounding in her chest, Michelle crouched down, expecting the inevitable shouts and flashes of torchlights to scan the area for intruders. But even after a minute, there was nothing to be heard. As she watched on, Charlotte carefully replaced the specimen jars in the back of the van, before closing and locking the door once again.

"Do you think we've gotten away with it?" asked Michelle, as they sauntered out into the sunlight again.

"I don't just think," replied Charlotte. "I know. We're the best in the business, you and I. This whole nonsense? It's child's play to people like us." She winked at Michelle, the kind of wink that made her weak at the knees and sent a flutter in her chest. If only Michelle had known then just how dangerous that wink would be. Falling for the enemy was always a risk in his job, and for the first time ever, Michelle worried she'd well and truly stumbled into the traps of dangerous love.

CHAPTER 13 – Surprise Sushi

Day: Monday
Time: 0730 hours
Location: Michelle's Apartment, Canberra

Michelle stirred peacefully in her slumber, opening her eyes and blinking them. She'd been having the most wonderful dream, that she'd pulled off the Trans-Global Trade Partnership without any further issues, and was being rewarded for her efforts in an official ceremony at Parliament House. Even as she blinked away the final tendrils of her imagination, she was filled with a sense of optimism and determination. In just over twenty-four hours from now, dignitaries and their representatives would be lining up at Government House, ready to sign the most important Trans-Global Trade Partnership ever put together in the history of humanity. It was a huge victory for Australia as a nation, but more importantly, for Michelle Morgan – both personally and professionally.

All she had to do now was babysit the deal, as they say in the business. In lay speak, it meant she was responsible for hosing down any last-minute jitters of concerns until the point where the deal was done and there was no backing down. Like most things in the negotiations industry, this was something easier said than done, but it only took one idiot to mouth off and say the wrong thing for it all to come tumbling down.

Showered and refreshed, Michelle made herself her morning coffee, and turned on the television, switching over to the Detritus News Breakfast program. It was then that her fantasies of glory were shattered, perhaps beyond repair.

"In breaking news from Canberra this morning, the Prime Minister Declan Martin has just announced that he will be reopening an Australian embassy in the North Korean capital, Pyongyang," announced the newsreader. He was an attractive young thing, with dark hair and a serious expression on his face. "We will be taking you live to the Prime Minister Martin's press conference any moment now."

Michelle was stunned. They had never discussed any level of trade with North Korea, and especially hadn't indicated reopening an embassy that had been closed for nearly forty years. Not only that, there had certainly never been any discussion as to whether they would be invited to join in with the Trans-Global Trade Partnership. In fact, Michelle knew they did all their trade through secret channels with other nations in their region.

But of one thing she was certain, Declan Martin was an old fool, but a fool playing with fire was too dangerous to ignore. Right now, in Parliament House, there would be a number of high-powered conversations going on between various Party members and factions, all of them grappling with the gravity of the Prime Minister's actions. But for Michelle, it was far closer to home for her. She glanced down at her phone, almost expecting it to blow up with a tsunami of incoming calls. No other nation in their right mind would seek to make a trade deal that just openly legitimised a rogue state like that. Michelle growled loudly. You don't do diplomacy by opening or closing embassies, especially not without consulting the wider audience.

It was as if she willed it to happen. Her phone started buzzing on the coffee table. It was Christopher Wayne.

"Michelle!" he yelled down the phone.

Michelle could almost hear the Foreign Minister's blood pressure skyrocketing.

"Have you seen the fucking news? That old geezer has fucked up royally this time! North fucking Korea! Do you have any idea what that means for us now?"

Michelle tried to remain calm. There was no situation, big or small, that her raw sexuality couldn't get them out from. Although, North Korea was a slightly bigger challenge than framing an Ambassador and a Chancellor for breaking and entering into the Prime Minister's office. "Nobody has contacted me yet to say they're out," she replied, hopeful that would be enough to soothe the Foreign Minister's nerves.

It wasn't.

"Well, I'll tell you what it bloody means! Japan is out! Tokyo called me just five minutes ago to say that they take an embassy in Pyongyang as an act of aggression, and have pulled out. Kaput, done. And if they pull out, who the knows how many other nations will pull out? This deal is falling apart right at the 11th hour."

Michelle remained silent. Japan were one of the first nations to guarantee supply of the Trans-Global Trade Partnership, and without them, the whole deal hung in the balance. Why couldn't that fool of a Prime Minister not simply wait two days – just two days – before he completely bombed Michelle's chances of success. "Shall we meet with the Japanese delegates together, Mr Wayne? We might be able to provide a level of reassurance to them."

Christopher Wayne pondered this for a few moments, and mulled it over in his mind. "Yes, Michelle, I think that is an excellent idea. Come by my office, and we can head over there together. I'll arrange for a driver to pick you up. Oh, and Michelle? Don't wear underwear."

The phone hung up, leaving Michelle slightly stunned. *Don't wear underwear.* She knew exactly what the Foreign Minister meant. The deal wasn't necessarily over, but Michelle Morgan would be going down one last time.

Michelle didn't even have the opportunity to get out of the car before Christopher Wayne got in. "Sir," she greeted, still unsure what the Minister had in mind for them. Sure, he'd been a negotiator in the past, but he was an old hat now, out of the game too long. Rather than keep his skills sharp, he'd used his considerable budget to outsource his jobs to others, and key negotiator was one of them.

"I have a plan for today," he said quietly, ensuring the driver wouldn't overhear them. "I'll negotiate the terms of any amendments to the original deal myself, but I need you to back me up where you can. And whatever happened today must stay strictly between us. Nobody else can know a thing. Not until I'm ready. Do you understand?"

"Yes, sir," replied Michelle. "Whatever you need me to do."

Christopher Wayne looked dolefully out the window as they drove around the monument that was at the heart of democracy in Australia. "I don't have to tell you, Michelle, but both of our future's are riding on this thing."

They remained silent for the remainder of the very short drive the Japanese Embassy. Pulling up outside, it reminded Michelle of an old portable classroom, and looked as though a simple breeze were sufficient to knock it over. Whoever was paying to have these Embassies built was clearly a cheapskate. At least the Japanese could afford a proper security team to give Michelle and Christopher a pat down, and send them through the metal detector.

Once through the security checkpoint, the pair were quickly escorted upstairs to the boardroom for an urgent meeting, which was already in progress by the time they arrived.

"Good morning, Mister Wayne and Madam Morgan. Please, sit," said the woman at the head of the table.

"The Ambassador," whispered Christopher as quietly as he could.

Despite the numerous meetings and negotiations Michelle had been part of during the early days of the deal, she'd always met with lower ranking officials, and never the Ambassador herself. It was a surprise for her to hear she had an Australian accent. Although, as part of her research, she'd become aware that the Ambassador had spent her formative years, through to her postgraduate degree in Mathematics in Australia.

"Madam Morgan," she continued, "It is a pleasure to meet you. I am Emiyo Nakamura, the Japanese Ambassador to Australia." Addressing both of them this time, she continued. "I must say, I am extremely distressed at the news Australia will open an embassy in North Korea. We already live in fear of their ballistics testing. They are an aggressor nation, an enemy of democracy and free trade across the globe, and this act of yours appears to condone their actions."

Christopher Wayne began talking. "I am deeply sorry, I was not even aware of these measures being taken, and I assure you, it was not in the plan. Unfortunately, the Prime Minister has gone a bit insane now. This was all his idea, but I assure you, there are members of the government trying to make him reconsider, right now as we speak."

Nakamura paused and looked deeply into Christopher's eyes. "We have a saying in Japan," she said. "A rotting fish always rots from the head."

After a moment of silence, Christopher closed his eyes, and remained silent for another moment. "Yes," he said deeply. "Yes, I agree. I offer you my assurance, that this Embassy – let's call it what it is – this embarrassment – will not go ahead. I guarantee it."

Michelle stiffened beside him, unsure what she could add to the narrative, other than nodding in agreement and acting as if she knew what was happening. What was Christopher's plan? Surely, he didn't have the power to override the Prime Minister, even if he was old and potentially senile. Unless he was hatching a plan to overthrow the Prime Minister, and launch a coup against Martin.

It was Nakamura's turn to pause and hum to herself. "Yes," she said finally. "We can accept this. I want your promise that an embassy will not open in North Korea, and I will sign your document tomorrow on behalf of the Government of Japan."

"You have my word," replied Christopher.

"Good," said Nakamura. "Now take off your clothes, please. It's lunch time."

Unquestioningly, Michelle and Christopher obliged, stripping completely naked before the Ambassador. If this was what it took to secure that deal, then it was what they were willing to do. After everything she'd done over the last few days, this was nothing for Michelle to turn her nose up at. The Ambassador walked over, and pinched Michelle's nipple, and cupped her breasts in her hand. She moved over and did the same to Christopher Wayne, cupping his genitals and jiggling his impressive set of testicles gently. After a moment, she appeared satisfied. "Excellent," she said. "Now do lie down on the table, both of you, on your backs. And stay still."

Michelle and Christopher did as they were told, laying flat on the boardroom table, looking upwards at the ceiling. It was just one thing after another these days, Michelle thought bitterly to herself. And now, she was being forced to take part in some sort of weird ritual, no doubt erotic in nature.

She didn't have to wait long before a man appeared over her, in traditional chef clothing. Michelle panicked for a moment, and wondered if this meant she was going to be eaten! *No, Michelle*, she told herself. *They don't eat people.* But what was the knife for? She closed her eyes, not wanting to see what they did to her. Something cold, wet and slimy was placed on her chest, in the cleavage between her perky breasts. Then another right beneath to it. After the fifth dot had been placed, Michelle opened her eyes and looked down. The chef was placing tradition sushi and nigiri on her body. Looking over, a second chef was doing exactly the same to Christopher Wayne. Minutes later, they were covered head to toe, mummified in sushi, more fish than human.

Michelle wanted to yell out, to ask *'what on earth is happening?'* but she didn't want to know what the punishment for knocking off one of the carefully prepared delicacies would be. At the very least, it would insult their host – or their captor, as the case may well be – which would be guaranteed to spell disaster for their trade deal.

With a clap from the Ambassador, the lights went down, and the room went dark. Another clap, and neon lights, blue and purple lit up the room again in an eerie, underwater glow. Her heart began to race. Whatever bizarre ritual this was, Michelle wanted no further part in it. But the fear of the unknown, and the desperation to prove herself against all odds kept her lying there, flat on her back, covered in raw fish and rice.

With a final clap from the Ambassador's hands, a door at the far end of the room opened up, and in single file, marching in perfect unison, came a group of Japanese businesswomen. Once they had surrounded the table, they bowed their heads to their guests, and took their seats. The one closest the Michelle avoided all eye contact, as though she were just another piece of the furniture.

Without warning, the Ambassador began speaking in rapid Japanese, either issuing orders, or chanting a prayer of sacrifice – Michelle couldn't tell which it was. Was the Trans-Global Trade Partnership really worth this level of humiliation? She silently cursed the Prime Minister, and swore an oath to herself, that if she ever got out of this situation, she would devote herself to tearing Declan Martin down, sparing him no mercy.

As she waited patiently for the end to come, a giant gong rang out, and without further warning, the businesswomen began pecking at the sushi on the naked Australians like ravenous seagulls fighting over a discarded box of chips. Though the chopsticks poked and prodded at her flesh, they did her no harm. She was even impressed when none of them tried to pick up her breasts or clitoris and bring those to their mouth, though she was certain several of them wanted to.

Once all the food had been consumed, the lights came back on again, blinding Michelle with their sheer brilliance. She closed her eyes tight again, blocking out the harshness of the fluorescent bulbs. Hadn't she suffered enough yet?

The group of women around them, clearly delighted by what the overhead lights revealed, clapped and cheered, whooping with delight. The Ambassador again spoke in rapid Japanese, and following another crash of the gong, the women rose from their seats, and filed out again, perhaps a little more eager than they'd filed in.

"Thank you, Mister Wayne, Madam Morgan, for your services. Those women that were here, they will be off to enjoy an orgy together. But I am not done with you yet – those women feasted on you, and now it is your turn to feast on me!" she announced dramatically, ripping off her entire outfit in one move, and throwing it to the side. Daring to open her eyes fully for the first time since the ordeal began, Michelle could see the Ambassador was fully naked, her small but beautiful breasts already engorging with erotic anticipation.

Climbing off the table, Michelle walked over, and kneeling before her like devout believer, she graciously began to lap at her vertical slit and clit with her tongue. Perhaps she was just grateful to be alive, but Michelle could swear she'd never had a better tasting pussy in her life. Christopher kissed her deeply on the mouth, and Nakamura reached down to start tugging on his growing cock. Whatever Mr Wayne was doing to the Ambassador, it was sending tremors through her body and down to his responsive clitoris. Nakamura's pussy throbbed violently in Michelle's mouth, threatening to erupt like Mount Fuji. Whatever this was, Michelle knew they had a responsibility to all other partied signing onto the trade deal, to pleasure the Japanese Ambassador in any way they could.

Nakamura pushed Michelle away from her, and in a single move, directed Christopher onto the table, on his back, legs dangling over the edge. She bent over, and began to suck at Christopher's cock, tasting the remnants of sushi and soy sauce. She was so graceful, Michelle thought. The way the nude Nakamura worked reminded her of the traditional theatre she'd seen in Osaka.

But there was no time to waste in reminiscing the past. Not when there was a whole future ahead of her, of only they could get through the next twenty-four hours unscathed. Renewed with the determination to succeed, Michelle began to work on Nakamura's ass – licking it gently as one would a peach, before reaching forward and masturbating her moist cunt with her hands. She was but the Ambassadors most humble servant, determined to please her, and her alone. Whatever she commanded, Michelle was willing to do.

Standing once more, Nakamura leaned backwards over the table, her long legs spread wide apart to reveal her hungry vagina. There was no denying her wish – *hopefully her final wish*, Michelle thought hotly.

"Fuck me, Michelle," she said simply, pointing to the wall where an enormous ceremonial ceramic dildo, painted with lotus flowers and cherry blossoms stood to attention.

Reaching for the thick, heavy implement, Michelle did as she was told, and pushed the cold glaze of the phallus against the entrance of Nakamura's cavern. With a prod and a thrust, she plunged it in further. There was no turning back now, not when she was mechanically fucking a Japanese diplomat. She wanted to fuck her so hard, the Australian government could open ten Embassies in Pyongyang and she wouldn't bat an eyelid.

But no. He was an old woman, at least forty-five, and Michelle had a responsibility to leave her undamaged. With short, shallow thrusts, she probed at her cervix. Like ringing a doorbell, the secret to opening a woman's pussy hole wider is by massaging her cervix – at least, that's what Michelle had learned by taking on several hundred different lovers. Just as always, the secret worked, and before she knew it, Michelle was on all fours, screwing Emiyo Nakamura while working her delicious clitoris with her tongue.

"Lower yourself onto my face," Nakamura demanded of Christopher Wayne. With a nimble leap and a subtle stumble, the Foreign Minister lowered his ass so it perched perfectly above the Ambassador's lips. Michelle turned her head. She didn't need to see what was going on in front of her. *Just focus on the task at hand.*

Moans filled the air after several minutes. "Fuck my mouth!" cried Emiyo, on the verge of orgasm. Christopher turned around, and as ordered, shoved his cock into Nakamura's open mouth and allowed her to perform oral sex on him. A wry smirk spread across his lips as he looked at Michelle, sweat dripping down his body from his efforts. He leaned in, and kissed Michelle hard on the mouth. They were nearly there, almost done now.

Michelle reached down, and with vigorous strokes of her fingers, masturbated the Japanese Ambassador's clit, until she gushed with a got stream of watery ejaculated all over the dildo and Michelle's hand. Christopher followed next, cumming over all over her face. Emiyo Nakamura had been perfectly bukkake'd by the Foreign Minister and his negotiations assistant.

After wiping herself down and redressing, Emiyo shook the hands of the Australians. "It was a pleasure, I assure you," she purred. "Now if I may, I have one more condition to add — I want you, Michelle, to fuck me annually, on this day, until the deal is no longer valid."

Christopher looked at Michelle as if to say 'don't you dare fuck this up for me, Morgan'.

She had no choice. If that's what it came down to, if that was what it took for the Japanese government to ignore the obvious mental instability of the Australian Prime Minister, then so be it. Michelle agreed to the terms of the arrangement.

"Do I really have to fuck her every year?" asked Michelle on their way back to Parliament House, each of them still reeking of fish and ejaculate.

"After what that woman put us though," replied the Foreign Minister, anger on his breath, "I'll be putting her on the first flight out of here as soon as that deal is signed."

CHAPTER 14 – The Signing of the Deal

Day: Tuesday
Time: 1130 hours
Location: Government House, Canberra

Government House always looked radiant in the late morning sunlight. The bright green lawns were dappled in the shadows of the pine trees that dotted the perimeter. A gathering was already in mid-swing by the time Michelle arrived for the historic signing of the Trans-Global Trade Partnership.

She brimmed with pride, chest swelling with satisfaction that after all the tension over the last few days, she'd finally succeeded in getting all the dignitaries and delegates together in one place to sign the deal. As she strode down the path towards the Foreign Minister, Michelle dreamed of a future for herself – enviable position, a pay rise, maybe even an allowance like all the other staffers. Anything was possible for her in this bright world.

"Congratulations, sir," greeted Michelle, extending her hand.

"Well done, Michelle," the Foreign Minister beamed in response. "I always had faith that you could pull this off."

Michelle smiled politely. "About that reward I was promised…"

"Hmmm, yes," Christopher replied before he could go on any longer. "Michelle, there's trouble brewing in the Government. After the Prime Minister's stunt yesterday, there are new developments that require my fullest attention. You'll get your reward, I assure you, but you'll just have to wait. We'll both have to wait."

There was something in his tone, Michelle could tell, that meant he was up to something. He was a man who held his cards to his chest, and today was no exception for Christopher Wayne. Although disappointed, Michelle knew she just needed to trust the Minister, trust he had a plan in place, and that she'd be justly rewarded when the time came. She just needed to have faith.

The representatives of all 27 signatories arrived one by one, with partners or lovers on hand, but as was the case for Brigitte and Hans, they arrived alone, and separately. Glancing around, Michelle noticed several dozen nervous eyes watching her, a mix of fear and hope that she would expose their affairs to their partners. But that simply wasn't Michelle's style – not unless she benefited personally from it. Even then, she wasn't one to break apart a marriage. She'd leave that job to the French Ambassadress.

Once the guests were formally escorted to their seats, the formal ceremony was underway. Christopher Wayne was the first to speak at the podium that had been set in place with a view of Lake Burley Griffin in the distance behind him. "I am proud to announce a new deal; a deal for today, and for tomorrow. A deal for trade and prosperity. A global deal."

His speech was long and slow, and interrupted numerous times by the sounds of delegates clapping and cheering. One by one, a representative from each nation was called up, asked to add their signature to the document, and return to their seat. The awaiting media rushed forward, photographing each of them with the intensity of a paparazzo trying to capture a troubled starlet at her worst. Each in turn smiled for the cameras, and spoke of what this deal meant for future generations of citizens, whether they be Italian, German, Guyanese or Japanese.

It was only once all the signatures had been added to the document that Michelle allowed herself a sigh of relief. There was absolutely nothing that could go wrong now. It was done, and finalised. And not a moment too soon, either.

The delegates were offered flutes of champagne and fine hors d'oeuvres while they gathered in small clusters around the formal garden. It all happened in a rush, and Michelle barely had time to take it in. The patio doors of the house swung open, and half a dozen police officers marched out, making a direct line for Brigitte and Hans, who were talking discretely behind a bush at the far corner of the lawn. With a yelp and a cry, the officers handcuffed the pair, and dragged them, kicking and screaming away from the celebration, never to be seen again. She smiled to himself. *Better them than me,* she thought devilishly.

"Howdy, partner," Charlotte said, greeting Michelle for the first time that day.

"Partner? You should know, I work alone," replied Michelle coyly.

Charlotte laughed. "If I remember correctly, we make a pretty good team, you and I. Anyway, Michelle – I have to go home to the States tonight. The President needs me to broker an important deal for him. It's complicated, I know, but I want you to come with me. You're one of the best in the business, and I need someone I can trust. And if that's someone I can fuck every now and then too…" She winked.

Michelle thought about the offer for a moment. She reflected on what it felt like to have Charlotte's naked body pressed against her own, the taste of her pussy on her lips, the way her body seized up when she came. She'd be a fool to let that all go, wouldn't she? She leaned in, and kissed the American, before clearing her throat to answer.

If you enjoyed International Relations (The Gender-Flipped Version), please consider leaving a review on Amazon or Goodreads. What may take you a minute or so means far, far more than that for independent authors such as myself.

I do hope to see you again in the next Parliamentary Desires (The Gender-Flipped Version) book, Congressional Proclivities.

Until we meet again,

H.G. Jones

CONGRESSIONAL PROCLIVITIES
The Gender-Flipped Version
Parliamentary Desires Book 2

Michelle Morgan is a busy contractor with a skill for negotiating major deals where all others fail. Following her successful negotiation of a global trade deal, she and her new ally, Charlotte Adams have been given a new task together. American President Geoffrey Nash has requested their assistance and expertise in negotiating important gun law reforms through the Congress.

It's a task that will take Michelle all the negotiation skills she has, taking her across the United States. Her adventure will introduce her to a range of larger-than-life characters, from the curious Gregory Miller, to Floridian alligator farmer, Roberta "Gator" Hill. But things are not all that they seem, and Michelle will need to develop some new skills, and quickly.

Follow Michelle and Charlotte as they negotiate the biggest gun law reform in American history, using their best tools for the job – their pussies.